For more than forty years,
Yearling has been the leading name
in classic and award-winning literature
for young readers.

Yearling books feature children's
favorite authors and characters,
providing dynamic stories of adventure,
humor, history, mystery, and fantasy.

Trust Yearling paperbacks to entertain,
inspire, and promote the love of reading
in all children.

The Mysteries of Spider Kane

Mary Pope Osborne

A YEARLING BOOK

For Bubba, Natalie, and Baby Mike — M.P.O.

Published by Yearling, an imprint of Random House Children's Books
a division of Random House, Inc., New York

Visit us on the Web! www.randomhouse.com/kids

**Educators and librarians, for a variety of teaching tools, visit us at
www.randomhouse.com/teachers**

ISBN: 978-0-440-42097-2

Printed in the United States of America

March 2006

10 9 8 7 6 5 4 3

CWO

Dear Readers,

I've always been afraid of large bugs and spiders. So when my husband and I bought a cabin in the woods of Pennsylvania years ago, I was unhappy to discover that there were lots of six- and eight-legged creatures sleeping in the corners and sometimes creeping across the floor.

One night I nearly fainted when I lifted a blanket off the sofa and saw the biggest spider I'd ever seen. It was nearly the size of a saucer! The spider heard my screams, jumped off the sofa, and vanished between the floorboards.

"We have to leave now and never come back," I told my husband.

"I don't think so," he said. (He didn't mind spiders at all.)

Well, if we weren't going to run away, I knew the only thing to do was to get over my fears. And the best way to do that was to learn more about what I was afraid of. So I went to the library and checked out a dozen books on bugs and spiders.

I'd planned to gather cold scientific information. But in the process, a number of bug names jumped off the page at me—leafwing butterflies, emperor moths, deathwatch beetles. I started making a list of all the names I liked, and a world of mystery and fantasy opened up. At the center was a remarkable detective named Spider Kane, who, in my mind, is that same scary creature I saw sitting on my sofa long ago.

He now invites you into his world…

Mary Pope Osborne

The last and least of things
That soar on quivering wings,
Or crawl among the grass blades out of sight
Have just as clear a right
To their appointed portion of delight
As queens or kings.

—Christina G. Rossetti

Spider Kane and the Mystery Under the May-Apple

CAST OF CHARACTERS
(in order of appearance)

PUPA LEAFWING—A middle-aged female butterfly; currently goes by name "La Mère"

LEON LEAFWING—Pupa Leafwing's son; a hotheaded, earnest young butterfly

MIMI—An attractive, gossamer-winged butterfly with a mysterious past

ROSIE—An energetic ladybug who caters for the Cottage Garden

LITTLE PICKLES—Rosie's companion; a good-natured ladybug who also caters for the Cottage Garden and makes tulip cradles for Garden babies

WALTER DOGTICK—Pupa Leafwing's former best friend; now an indigent scavenger

SPIDER KANE—Retired captain from the Mosquito Wars, theater director, jazz musician, and amateur detective

MIDGE APPLEWORM—A middle-aged, wealthy matron

LOU SALAMANDER and NYMPH LATELL—Members of the Women's Bug Club

COLONEL APPLEWORM (Ret.)—Midge's husband, nicknamed "Tubby"

DR. T. K. ANT—Head librarian of the National Ant Archives

MAJOR GENERAL ROBERT "BOB" BUM—Steward of the queen and deputy treasurer of Bee City

SERGEANT THOMAS HAWKINS—A burned-out moth nicknamed "the Hawk"; one of the emperor's henchmen

MARGARET—Mimi's mother; an aged gossamer-winged butterfly

EMPEROR MOTH—Ruler of the Island of the Dark Swamp

A few mosquitoes; hordes of grubs

PART I

❧ ONE ❧

Thunder rumbled in the distance. The sky above the abandoned Cottage Garden was dark gray. As the summer breeze blew the tall weeds and flowers, tiny butterfly voices came from inside a broken geranium pot.

"There's that tacky thing again," said La Mère Leafwing, peering outside.

Leon Leafwing looked up from his book and gazed at his mother. "What tacky thing?"

"There. Over by the Appleworms' pot."

Leon squinted at the gossamer-winged butterfly hovering near Colonel and Mrs. Appleworm's flowerpot. She wore a blue iridescent gown and dark glasses. "Wow, she looks wonderful," he breathed.

"Wonderful?" La Mère snorted. "I saw her

yesterday near the Lily Pond. She was embracing some horrible-looking creature. He had a red bandanna around his head and—"

"Look," interrupted Leon. "She dropped something—she doesn't seem to realize it. She's starting to take off—"

"Stay right where you are, dearie," said La Mère. "She's no good. I'm telling you I saw her—"

Before his mother could finish, Leon soared out of the geranium pot and zoomed over to the Appleworms'. He scooped up a tiny purple silk scarf, then darted as fast as he could after the gossamer-winged butterfly.

"Excuse me..." he called, but she didn't seem to hear him. He flew alongside her, and just as he reached out to tap her, she turned.

"Help!" she screamed, flailing her arms wildly.

Leon ducked and managed to cover his head. "Your scarf!" he shouted. "Your scarf!"

She stopped in midair. "What?"

"You dropped your scarf!"

"Oh!" The gossamer-winged butterfly lit

down in the tall meadow flowers. "Goodness, were you just trying to return my scarf?" she asked, panting.

"Yes," said Leon. And he handed over the tiny piece of purple silk.

"Oh, I'm so sorry. Will you forgive me for being so stupid?"

"You're forgiven; no harm done. What's your name?"

"They call me Mimi," she said. She took off her sunglasses. And Leon saw traces of sorrow and fear in her dark, lovely eyes. "And you?"

"Leon. Leon Leafwing."

"Oh, what a good name. Leon Leafwing. It sounds so brave and reassuring."

Before Leon could speak, a clap of thunder cracked the sky.

"Help!" Mimi screamed, throwing herself into Leon's arms. She was trembling like a leaf.

"It's only thunder," he said softly.

"I'm sorry, Leon," she said. Then to his surprise, she began weeping. "But I'm so afraid…" she whispered.

"What are you afraid of?"

"I can't tell you. I can't tell anyone."

"You can tell me."

"Well…" Mimi sniffed and looked into his eyes. "No, I don't want to get you involved. You're too nice. I must be going."

"Mimi, wait—"

"Please, I must go."

"Let me fly you home before it starts to rain. I daresay I can go a bit faster. Come on, climb on my back. Where do you live?"

"In the Wildflower Woods under a May-apple."

Leon heard a deep, rasping cough coming from behind the rosemary hedge. "Shhh! Did you hear something?" he asked Mimi.

"Yes! No! I don't know!" she stammered, trembling with terror. "Help me, Leon. Please, take me home quickly!"

"Wait, wait. Let me take a look." Leon started toward the hedge.

"No, Leon! We must go *now!*"

The panic in Mimi's voice brought Leon back to her. She climbed on his back, and he took off swiftly, carrying her away from the Flowerpot District to the Wildflower Woods in the northeast corner of the Cottage Garden.

It was just starting to rain when they arrived at Mimi's little burrow under an umbrella-like May-apple plant. The burrow was made of mud and straw. It had a pebble terrace and a wooden door with a pine-needle doormat.

"Thank you for bringing me home," Mimi said, sounding somewhat calmer. "Would you like to come in for some tea and strawberry until the rain stops?"

"Sure, that would be nice."

As Mimi led Leon through the front door of her burrow, he thought he heard the mysterious cough again. And when he glanced back over his shoulder, he felt sure he saw something move behind a mound of dead leaves.

"Leon? Is something wrong?" asked Mimi.

"No, no, nothing. Nothing at all," he said, trying to sound nonchalant, for he did not want to alarm her again.

❧ TWO ❧

"Please, have a seat," Mimi offered, and she guided Leon to a small twig chair. She lit a beeswax candle, then poured rainwater from a hickory barrel into a tiny stone kettle. Leon glanced about at the bare earthen floor, empty walls, and bed of straw.

"Forgive the look of my place," she said, putting the kettle on a beeswax burner. "But I only moved to the Garden a few days ago."

"I guess that's why I've never seen you before," said Leon. "My mother's noticed you, though. She saw you yesterday near the Lily Pond with a—a sort of odd-looking creature."

"Oh, that wasn't me!" said Mimi. She sounded upset again. "I was here all day yesterday."

"Hmm, well, she must have been mistaken, then," said Leon quickly. Anxious to change the subject, he looked around the room and caught sight of three dusty books lying on her bed. "My, don't these look interesting?" he said, flitting over to them.

13

"Oh! Those!" Before Leon could touch the books, Mimi darted to the bed and scooped them up. "They're nothing, really."

"Well, what—what are their titles?"

Mimi peered at the book spines. "Um—*Ants at War, Ants at Peace, Ants Forever.* Really, they're not very good."

"But they look so old. Are they rare?"

"Oh, no, no, no. I just picked them up at a flea market. Ah-choo! Goodness, they're so dusty—let me move them out of our way."

Leon was puzzled as Mimi fluttered to the back of her burrow with the books. When she was out of sight, he quickly peeked out the window and studied her yard. He saw no signs of the coughing prowler.

"There," Mimi said, returning. She lifted her little kettle from the burner. Her hands seemed to be trembling as she poured the steamy rainwater into two buttercups filled with lemon grass.

Leon watched her, trying to figure out what was troubling the beautiful butterfly. "Where'd you live before?" he asked.

"Far away…on an island," she said.

"Really? Where?"

"I think I'd rather not talk about it, if you don't mind," she said, looking at him sadly. "The past brings back some painful memories, Leon."

"Oh, of course." As Mimi cut two slices from a strawberry, Leon felt anger at the thought that anyone or anything would cause her pain. She seemed so nice.

She placed the tiny pieces of the fruit on the delicate petals of a sweet white violet, then served Leon. "Do you live alone?" she asked.

"No, I live with my mother—or 'La Mère,' as she calls herself these days."

"La Mère? It sounds French. Is she from France?"

"Far from it. She grew up in the Goatweed Patch next to Dogtick's place—a fact that she tries to hide."

"Really? Why?"

"I guess because she wants everyone in the snobby Flowerpot District to like her. She wants to be part of the 'in' crowd."

"Where's the Flowerpot District?"

"Where you dropped your scarf. We live between the Appleworms and the Salamanders. My mother'll do anything to be accepted by them. She's even given up flying and tries to walk, like the Salamanders. But she keeps falling again and again—sometimes hits her head."

"Oh, how sad."

"It is, rather."

"Leon, guess what falls down and never gets hurt."

"What?"

"Snow!"

As Leon chuckled, Mimi slapped her little knees and laughed a lovely, tinkling laugh. It touched Leon to see her happy for a moment. But then sorrow returned to her face. "You know, there was a time when I wanted to be accepted by everyone too," she said softly.

"Really?"

"Oh, yes. I prayed for yellow wings instead of blue. I never laughed because I didn't like my high little titter. I even—" She stopped.

"You what?" said Leon.

"I wore three pairs of dance tights so my legs wouldn't look so skinny."

"No kidding?" said Leon. "Me too. I mean I stopped wearing short-sleeved shirts because I thought my arms were too skinny."

"Oh, Leon, your arms are wonderful."

"Thank you," said Leon. He was amazed; he'd never had a conversation like this before.

"You know, some bad experiences have taught me that being yourself is the best thing in the world to be," said Mimi. "Only sometimes you're forced—" She shook her head as tears flooded her eyes.

"What's wrong, Mimi?" said Leon.

"Nothing." She smiled sadly, then began singing in her high little voice:

> *If you can't be yourself, friend,*
> *What's the point of living?*
> *If you can't be yourself, friend,*
> *You might as well give in.*

Leon could hardly speak. "Did you make that song up just now?" he asked with wonder.

She nodded.

"But that's the best song I ever heard."

"Oh." She smiled with embarrassment. "I guess you inspire me, Leon."

They held each other's gaze for a long moment. Then she whispered, "Would you like to see something very special?"

Leon nodded, enthralled.

"I really shouldn't show you this, but you won't tell anyone. Will you?"

"No, no."

"Good. I'll be right back. Close your eyes."

Leon did as he was told. His heart did soft, fluttery things as he inhaled the fresh scent of lemon tea and listened to the rain pattering on the thatched roof of the little burrow.

"You can open your eyes now," Mimi said, returning to him.

When Leon looked up, he was struck by a dazzling light coming from the top of her head. "Goodness," he breathed. "What's that?"

"Shhh. A diamond crown," she whispered. "Can you sing, Leon?"

"No, not really."

"Oh, I bet you sing beautifully. I can tell from

your speaking voice. Please sing for me."

Leon laughed nervously. Then he cleared his throat and began crooning in a lovely bass:

> *Some enchanted evening,*
> *You may see a stranger,*
> *You may see a stranger*
> *Across a crowded room...*

As he sang, Mimi began to dance.

With the tiny diamond crown sparkling on her head, she tiptoed gracefully around her burrow. Her blue iridescent wings fluttered up, then down, her cares and troubles seeming to fall away from her. She moved so perfectly in time with the melody that Leon felt as if they were both singing and both dancing. When she began to twirl around, he lifted his voice and sang as he'd never sung before:

> *And somehow you know,*
> *You know even then*
> *That somewhere you'll see her*
> *Again and again.*

❧ THREE ❧

Leon was bursting with happiness as he told his mother about the visit with Mimi. "And not only is she a great dancer, but she tells jokes and makes up songs. She invited me over on Saturday to help her build some shelves. She can't afford to spend any money on her place now—" He stopped to catch his breath.

La Mère was not impressed. She fanned herself with a ginkgo leaf as she lay stretched out on her velvety cattail sofa. "Don't be silly, dearie. She's not interested in you."

"What?"

"I told you yesterday I saw her hugging some horrible-looking bug. He was wearing a dirty red thing on his head and had an ugly patch over his eye."

"And I told you that you were wrong," said Leon, though not very confidently. "She said it wasn't her, and I believe her."

"Phooey, I've got good eyes, sonny. I know what I see. Furthermore, isn't she quite a bit older than you?"

"No—well, maybe just a little—but that doesn't matter."

"What kind of butterfly arrives penniless in town, Leon, and rents a burrow by herself in the Wildflower Woods? Whew!" La Mère fanned harder.

"*My* kind of butterfly!"

"Stop being silly. What will my friends think if they see you with her?"

"WHO CARES?"

"I care! She's a cheap little nobody!"

"How can you say that?" said Leon, hopping up and down with rage. "She's one of the nicest, kindest butterflies I've ever met. She's got troubles, and she needs friends—and you insult her!"

"Leon, Leon, I just want something better for you. What about Muffy Salamander?"

"I hate Muffy Salamander! I hate all the snobs who live around here!" Leon shrieked. "I'm going to see Mimi on Saturday! And if you don't like it, I'll move out."

"Well, I don't like it," said La Mère.

"Fine. Good. Then I'm leaving." And having said that, Leon soared out of La Mère's cracked geranium pot, without even a glance back.

Leon left the Flowerpot District and flew swiftly to the middle of the Cottage Garden. There, near the stone birdbath, was the snug little home of his best friends, Rosie and Little Pickles. The two ladybugs lived in a tiny cottage under a moonflower vine.

Though a bit slow and clumsy on the wing, Rosie and Little Pickles had wonderful, energetic personalities. They earned their living making tulip cradles for the Garden babies and catering picnics and parties.

When Leon peeked in their kitchen window, he caught them wearing their matching polka-dotted dresses with pink aprons. Though the birchwood walls and floor were scrubbed bone white, the kitchen was in its usual disarray. Tiny copper saucepans, soup pots, and muffin tins were stacked everywhere. Bouquets of dried thyme, mint, and basil hung from the low ceiling.

Jars filled with pickles, sauces, and relishes crowded the countertops.

At the moment, the two ladybugs were making pies. As Rosie pressed some dough down into one of five acorn caps, she called to Little Pickles, "Don't forget the cinnamon!"

"I won't," said Little Pickles, sprinkling the brown powder over peach slices and blueberries in a walnut mixing bowl.

"Oh, and don't forget the nutmeg—" said Rosie.

"Hi!" said Leon, poking his head through their window.

The two ladybugs screamed.

"Gracious!" said Little Pickles, shaking her spoon at him. "I'm going to beat you with this!"

"I'll throw dough in your face next time you scare us like that, Leafy!" said Rosie, calling Leon by his nickname. Rosie nicknamed everyone. Long ago she'd started calling her friend Bess "Little Pickles" because Bess made the best pickles in the Garden.

"Just in time. We're making blueberry-peach

pie!" Little Pickles said.

"Oh. Great," said Leon without enthusiasm.

"All righty, let's spoon that in here now," said Rosie to Little Pickles. Together, they piled the filling into the five pie shells, then drizzled lemon juice and butter over it.

Little Pickles slipped the acorn pie plates into a clay oven as Rosie licked the spoon.

"Mmm-mmm!" Rosie said, her eyes wide. "Here, Leafy, *you* can lick the bowl."

"No thanks. I'm not very hungry."

"*What?* Not lick the bowl! Little Pickles, he must be sick."

Before Leon could say another word, Rosie and Little Pickles yanked off their aprons. They grabbed Leon and led him into their sun-dappled sitting room. They pushed him onto a feather-stuffed corn-husk sofa, then plopped down beside him.

"Now," said Rosie. "What's wrong?"

Leon sighed. "I have a new friend named Mimi, but my mother doesn't like her, and we just had a terrible fight, and now I don't have any place to live, and—"

"Whoa, whoa," said Rosie. "One thing at a time. First, you can live here with us."

"Of course," said Little Pickles.

Leon smiled, touched by their kindness.

"Second—tell us *all* about this Mimi."

As the three friends sat close to one another in the warm afternoon light, Leon told the ladybugs about meeting the gossamer-winged butterfly. He told them how Mimi seemed sad and frightened. He told them about the strange cough behind the hedge. He told them all about her burrow, her snow joke, and her odd and wonderful little song. He almost told them about the secret diamond crown, but he stopped himself just in time. He did mention, however, that Mimi danced like a diamond sparkling in the dawn.

When he finished, Rosie and Little Pickles just stared at him. "Gracious," said Little Pickles.

"His first girlfriend," whispered Rosie.

"*Girlfriend?* She's not my *girlfriend*," said Leon. "I don't even know her, and she's older than me. She's not a *girlfriend*. She's just a friend."

"Sure," said Rosie. She stared wistfully into

the distance and imitated Leon—"And she dances like a diamond sparkling in the dawn."

"Cut it out," said Leon. "She's new in town, that's all. I'm trying to be a good citizen and make her feel welcome."

"Leon! Leon!" came a voice from outside.

"What?" Leon fluttered to the door.

"Come here, you brat! You can't just move out like that!" Using a leaf-stem cane, La Mère was hobbling down a molehill toward the cottage.

"Leafy, look! Your mom's walking," said Rosie, peering out the window.

"She's pathetic," said Leon. "She's trying to walk like the Salamanders." He charged outside. "Mother, what in the world are you doing here?"

"I want you to come home! Now!" said La Mère.

"Forget it. I'm staying here until you accept Mimi into our lives."

"Accept Mimi into our lives!" La Mère waved her walking cane. "This is not an opera, Leon! This is real life. You can't just go around making

friends with the first tacky oddball who comes along."

"Tacky oddball? That's disgusting!" said Leon. "You can't talk about Mimi that way."

"I can, dearie, because I have your own best interests at heart. And if you don't come home now, I'll have to take action."

"What sort of action, ma'am?" called Rosie.

"Horrible action, dearie!" said La Mère, pointing her cane at Rosie. "Horrible, horrible, horrible action."

"Well, take action!" said Leon. "Take it right home with you!"

"You'll be sorry," said La Mère. "Remember, you only get one mother in this world!" With that, she turned and started hobbling back the way she'd come.

"Why don't you fly, Mother?" Leon shouted after her. "Butterflies are supposed to fly!"

"NO! They're supposed to mind their mothers!" And with that, La Mère disappeared over the crest of the molehill.

"Mimi's my girlfriend, Mother!" shouted

Leon. "Get that? *My girlfriend!*"

"Gracious," said Little Pickles as Leon collapsed on the cornhusk sofa.

"We didn't know you had it in you, dearie," said Rosie.

✜ FOUR ✜

All Leon could think about that week was Mimi. Mimi, Mimi, Mimi. Finally on Saturday, in the early morning mist, he collected a tiny bouquet of silver thyme. Little Pickles gave him a jar of watermelon pickles, and Rosie tied a tiny peach-colored ascot around his neck. Then Leon waved good-bye to his two best friends and took off for Mimi's burrow in the Wildflower Woods.

He felt light with joy as he sailed over the hazy Cottage Garden—over the stone birdbath, over the Lily Pond, the old sundial, and the meadow rue. But as he fluttered close to the Wildflower Woods, he realized he was quite early. Mimi wasn't expecting him until noon. So he lit down under a lilac bush to rest for a while.

Leon plucked a purple flower and put it in the buttonhole of his jacket. He straightened his little ascot. Sitting peacefully in the fragrant shade, he began dreaming about his future with Mimi for the hundredth time that week. Perhaps one day they'd marry in Bee City, where the most beautiful weddings took place. Perhaps he'd even sing their song at the wedding. He took a deep breath, then began in his gentle bass:

>*Some enchanted evening,*
>*When you find your true love,*
>*When you feel her call you*
>*Across a crowded room,*
>*Then fly to her side —*

But his song was interrupted by loud, ugly laughter. "Dumb enchanted cheese dog," sang a mocking voice.

When Leon whirled around, he saw Walter Dogtick standing nearby in the bristle grass, clutching a big sack.

"Hello, Leon, little son of *La Mère*," Walter said sarcastically. "How 'bout this for a love song":

Dogtick, Leafywing, Dogtick, Leafywing,
   Why can't a Dogtick dance with a Leafywing?

As the old tick sang, he danced a clumsy little dance. Leon felt sorry for him. Walter Dogtick had been hurt and angry ever since Pupa Leafwing had changed her name to "La Mère" and moved from the Goatweed Patch to the Flowerpot District. Though they'd been best friends when they were young, La Mère now refused to recognize Dogtick in public.

"How's that for a real love song?" said Walter.

"Fine, Wally."

"You know, Leon, I knew your mother when she was just a fat little caterpillar."

"I know, Wally."

The old tick chuckled and tugged on his dirty old sack. "Well, I got something that will get her back now," he said.

Leon saw a tiny piece of purple cloth sticking out of the opening of the sack. "What's in there?" he asked Dogtick.

"Wouldn't *you* like to know?" Walter said.

"Okay. Look, I'm not bothering you, Wally,"

said Leon. "So why don't you just move along?"

Walter Dogtick laughed loudly. Then, dragging his soiled sack behind him, he crept off, singing:

> Dogtick, Leafywing, Dogtick, Leafywing,
> Why can't a Dogtick dance with a Leafywing?

As the crude voice faded away, Leon shuddered. The lonely Dogtick depressed him. He fluffed up his ascot, picked up the thyme bouquet and watermelon pickles, then fluttered into the air.

As soon as Leon soared above the wild strawberries and pink pasture roses, his good spirits returned. Gliding toward Mimi's burrow, he pictured them someday living in a little burrow of their own. Perhaps it would be carpeted with corn silk. A tuft of lavender would be their bed. Their home would always be warm and cozy and filled with the scent of lemon tea.

He was smiling as he landed near the Mayapple.

It was a long moment before he realized something terrible had happened. At first, he simply stared at the caved-in burrow: the ugly mounds of dirt littered across the ground, the scattered straw, pebbles, and pine needles.

"Mimi?" he called in a frightened voice.

Horror filled him as he stared at the torn pages of her books, and her twig chairs broken in half.

Then he heard someone cough behind the bushes. "Who's there?" He darted to the brush. The grass rustled, but there was no sign of anyone.

Dazed, Leon rushed back to the wreckage. He threw aside the twigs and straw, expecting to find his friend among the ruins. But all he found was her little dark glasses.

"MIMI!" he screamed.

❧ FIVE ❧

The fragrance of night-blooming moonflower filled Rosie and Little Pickles's kitchen. And as a cool breeze blew through their window, the cream-colored curtains rose and fell like ghosts.

"Calm down, Leafy," said Rosie when Leon had finished his terrible story. "I'm sure she's still alive."

"How can you be sure?" Leon cried. Wearing Mimi's dark glasses, he was fluttering frantically about the kitchen.

"For one thing, you'd have found her body among the wreckage if she'd been killed."

"That's right." Little Pickles nodded.

"Then where is she?" said Leon. "What happened to her? I flew everywhere looking for her. I asked at the Lily Pond, the Flowerpots, the stone wall—everywhere!"

"Did you consider that she might have been kidnapped?" said Rosie.

"Kidnapped?"

"Yes."

Leon stopped fluttering. "No, I didn't think of that. Wait a minute, wait a minute." He sat and stared at Rosie. "She *was* kidnapped. Yes, she was! And I know exactly who did it."

"Who?" said Rosie and Little Pickles.

"Walter Dogtick," said Leon. "I saw Walter

Dogtick coming from the Wildflower Woods just before I got to Mimi's. He was carrying a sack. A big one—big enough to hold Mimi! And I saw something purple sticking out of it. Mimi's scarf!" Leon nearly choked with excitement. "It was her scarf! She was…"

"Oh, Leafy, *stop it*," said Rosie. "Dogtick always carries that dirty old sack. He's a scavenger. He likes to collect junk. You know that."

"No, no! This is too much of a coincidence! That's it! That's it!" Leon pounded the table, knocking over sauce bottles and pie plates.

"Honey, stop," said Rosie. "Get ahold of yourself. And take off those ridiculous sunglasses."

Leon heaved a great sigh. He took off Mimi's dark glasses, revealing his red, teary eyes. "Then where is she?" he asked in a small voice. "I looked everywhere."

"We know you did, sweetie," said Little Pickles.

"Look, before you fly off and accuse anyone, maybe we should try to get some help," said Rosie.

"Who can help us?" said Leon.

"I don't know."

"Wait," said Little Pickles in a low, whispery voice. "I have an idea."

"What?"

"Maybe we should go see Spider Kane, Rosie."

A smile slowly crossed Rosie's face. "Of *course*. Why didn't I think of that?"

"Who's Spider Kane?" said Leon.

"He's amazing, Leon," said Little Pickles. "I've never met him, but Rosie's told me all about him."

"Spider Kane's an old friend of mine. I served with him in the Mosquito Wars," said Rosie.

"He was wounded in battle," said Little Pickles excitedly. "Two of his legs are crippled, but he still gets around quite remarkably. He travels all over the world!"

"Not only does he travel, he's also a fine jazz musician," said Rosie.

"He plays the clarinet!" said Little Pickles.

"Yes, and he composes music, and he writes

and directs plays in his spare time."

"Well, a traveling jazz musician playwright is not what we need now," said Leon.

"Oh, but he's also a brilliant detective!" said Little Pickles.

"Is he ever!" said Rosie.

"Really?" said Leon. "Then why haven't I ever heard of him?"

"Since he moved into the Cottage Garden last autumn, Spy's been—that's my nickname for him, it's short for Spider—anyway, he's been..."

"A bit of a hermit, right, Rosie?" said Little Pickles.

"Oh, yes, that's a good way to put it."

"He mentioned he was writing a new play or something, didn't he, Rosie?" said Little Pickles.

"I thought you said you'd never met him," Leon said to Little Pickles.

"She hasn't," said Rosie quickly. "I told her all these things. Yes, Spy's been very busy and reclusive."

"Well, let's not disturb him, then," said Leon.

"Oh, no, no, no. I think we *should* disturb him," said Little Pickles.

"Of course we should!" said Rosie. "Spy loves a mystery. How about it, Leon?"

"Well, okay. But I don't know—"

"Don't worry," said Rosie. "I promise you that whatever happens, you won't be sorry. I'm sure you've never met anyone like Spider Kane in your whole life."

As Leon flew through the windy dark with Rosie and Little Pickles clinging to his back, strange sounds filled his ears. It was as if the wind rustling through the grass were gossiping about the evil that had happened under the May-apple.

She's gone, gone, never see her again,
Never, never, never, never, never…

"No!" cried Leon. But his voice could not be heard above the mad whisperings of the night.

PART II

❧ SIX ❧

"I think I've found it! I hear music!" Rosie shouted as she led the way along the crumbling stone wall, searching for the entrance to Spider Kane's home.

Leon and Little Pickles followed her into a tiny, cavelike hollow between two stones. Then they groped their way down a dark tunnel that led to the elegant chambers of Spider Kane.

They found him playing a jazz tune on a clarinet made from a hollow river reed. The lively music moved in time with a leaping candle flame, and shadows danced on the chalky stone walls and silken floor. Beside the spider was a briarwood pipe and a golden goblet made from a touch-me-not flower. Around his shoulders was a paisley dressing gown.

When the jazzy song ended, Rosie spoke softly: "Spy?"

Spider Kane jerked around to face his three visitors. Then he burst into laughter. "Lieutenant Rose! Good heavens!"

The two hugged each other warmly. Then Rosie said, "Spy, I'd like you to meet two dear friends, Little Pickles and Leon Leafwing—"

"Hello, Miss Pickles! What a pleasure," said Spider Kane in his deep, velvety voice.

"Gracious," said Little Pickles, trembling with excitement.

As Spider Kane turned to him, Leon quickly slipped on Mimi's dark glasses to hide his teary, swollen eyes.

"Hello, Mr. Leafwing, very pleased to meet you, too," said Spider Kane.

"Thank you. You can call me Leon."

"Fine, Leon. Now sit! All of you, sit and let me get you something to drink!" Spider Kane moved across the room with a slight limp. Then he poured a dark red liquid into three golden touch-me-not goblets. "Vintage cherry juice," he said. "How about some dinner? Parsnip pie? Peas in pastry shells?"

"No thank you, Mr. Kane," said Little Pickles. "We've already eaten."

"Ah, yes, I see that now. You dined on black bean soup."

"How did you know?" stammered Little Pickles.

"I've studied food stains for many years, Miss Pickles," he said. "The dark blotches on your blouse are definitely black bean soup."

"Oh, dear," said Little Pickles, blushing and putting her hand over the stains.

Rosie laughed. "I see you haven't lost your touch, Spy."

"No indeed, Lieutenant Rose."

"Good," said Rosie. "Because we need your help tonight. Leon is in great distress."

"Ah." The spider fixed his eyes on the butterfly. "Would you kindly remove your glasses, sir?"

When Leon took off Mimi's dark glasses, Spider Kane stared at his red eyes. "Your girlfriend," the spider said softly.

"How did you know?"

"Your tear-stained face speaks a thousand words, Leon. As does the wilted lilac in your buttonhole. I assume you paid a call on her—and she wasn't there?"

"That's right," said Leon sadly. "Her books were torn apart, her furniture was broken. I just found these little glasses—"

"Ah, let me see." Spider Kane took the dark glasses from Leon and studied them. "But the gossamer-winged lady was missing," he said quietly.

Leon gasped. "How—how did you know she was a gossamer-winged butterfly?"

"I have the rare gift of being able to make instant and perfect calculations of size without the use of a measuring tool," said Spider Kane. "I can tell you that these dark glasses exactly fit the head of a gossamer-winged butterfly."

"You know the head size of a gossamer-winged butterfly?"

"I know the head sizes of over two hundred different kinds of butterflies, my friend. If these belonged to a butterfly in your family, they'd be half a micrometer larger."

As Leon laughed with astonishment, Spider Kane smiled and lit his pipe.

❧ SEVEN ❧

Spider Kane was silent when Leon finished the story of how he'd met Mimi. He puffed on his pipe and stared at the flickering candle flame, deep in thought. "So," he said finally, "the sky was overcast when she dropped the silk scarf near the Appleworms' pot?"

"Yes, that's right."

"Yet she was wearing dark glasses?"

"Well, yes…"

"And you thought you heard someone cough behind a bush?"

"Yes, and I felt as if we were being watched. I heard the same coughing noise outside her home."

"Hmm. And you say that she seemed quite

anxious? As if she were afraid that someone might be following her?"

"Yes," said Leon.

Spider Kane nodded, then took a sip from his golden goblet. "Did you see any items of interest in her burrow? Anything someone might want to steal?"

"Well…she'd just moved in, and she didn't have many things. She seemed quite penniless, in fact."

"So there was nothing there?"

"Just some old books from a flea market."

"What kind of books?"

"Um—it was a trilogy of ant novels."

"*Yes?*" Spider Kane leaned forward, his eyes burning with interest. "Are you certain, Leon?"

"Yes. Why?"

"Nothing." The spider bit his thin lip and settled back in his chair. He relit his pipe and puffed hard. "Go on. What else? What else did you see?"

"Nothing, really."

"You're not telling the truth, Leon."

"I'm not?"

"No. When butterflies lie, they often glance to the left, as you just did."

"Oh." Leon shifted uncomfortably. He hated breaking Mimi's confidence.

"Yes?" said Spider Kane. "What are you concealing?"

"Well." Leon took a deep breath. "She did have a tiny little crown in her possession."

"Crown? What kind of crown?"

"Um—a diamond crown."

"Good heavens!" The spider jerked forward. "Did it not strike you as odd that a penniless butterfly would have a diamond crown?"

"Well, yes, it did, but..."

"But? But?"

"Well, I...um...she danced and I sang...and it..." Leon swallowed, overcome with embarrassment. "It didn't occur to me to ask..." He stopped. It was impossible to explain that magic moment with Mimi wearing her crown.

"I see," said Spider Kane softly.

An awkward silence filled the room.

"Well!" said Spider Kane. "What else can you tell me, son?"

"Uh…well…I know Rosie thinks I'm wrong about this, but…"

"Yes?" said Spider Kane.

"I don't want to point the blame at anyone, but…"

"Yes? Yes?"

"I did see Walter Dogtick coming from the Wildflower Woods a moment before I got to Mimi's. He was dragging a sack. And I saw a tiny piece of purple cloth sticking out of it."

"Yes? So?"

"Well, Mimi had a purple scarf, see. So I wondered if maybe she could—well, might possibly have been inside that sack."

"Good heavens, I hope not," said Spider Kane. He pulled off his paisley dressing gown and grabbed his trench coat and fedora. "It's time I visited the scene of the crime," he said. "Get your hats, my friends!"

Since none of them wore hats, their departure was immediate.

✌ EIGHT ✌

The Wildflower Woods sparkled with dewdrops. In the pale light of dawn, Spider Kane, Leon, Rosie, and Little Pickles stared at the wreckage under the May-apple. Though he hadn't slept all night, Leon felt very alert as he waited for Spider Kane's conclusions.

At first the spider was silent, only nodding to himself. Then suddenly he was limping about everywhere—touching this, examining that, missing nothing. "Aha!" he shouted, crouching and digging in the dirt.

"What?" cried Leon.

"Aha!" he shouted again.

"Gracious, what is it, Mr. Kane?" said Little Pickles.

"Ah." The spider came to a halt and stared at the ground. After a long pause he rose from his crouching position and lit his pipe. "There was much fighting and struggle," he said. "I see wing tracks everywhere. Also—the diamond crown you mentioned, Leon, is nowhere to be found."

"Oh, that's right," said Leon. He fluttered above the wreckage again. "And I don't see Mimi's silk scarf, either. Only the books are still here. But oh—look at this!"

The others hurried over.

"There're only two books!" he said, pointing to the torn pages of the Ant Trilogy, lying on the ground, flipping in the breeze. "See—*Ants at Peace* and *Ants Forever*. There was another one, a third book! Where is it?"

"Good question." Spider Kane stroked his chin and began combing through the wreckage again.

"He's right, Spy," said Rosie. "There're only two books."

"What can that mean, Mr. Kane?" said Little Pickles.

Spider Kane didn't answer. He was gaping at the dirt floor beneath the May-apple. "Good heavens," he said under his breath. Then he crouched down and gingerly touched the ground. As the others rushed to see what he was doing, he shouted, "Stop! Stop! Or you'll

49

destroy the remaining letters."

"What letters?" said Rosie.

"There's a message scratched into the dirt here," he said.

"What does it say?" cried Leon.

"See for yourself. Unfortunately, much of it has been wiped out, perhaps in the struggle between Mimi and her assailant."

As Leon fluttered close to the ground, he read:

HE   R MOTH ENDS THE D

"What does it mean?" he cried.

But suddenly he heard a cough coming from the woods. Before Leon could speak, Spider Kane rushed toward the brush. "Halt!" he shouted. Leon's heart pounded as the spider shouted, "Come out! Show yourself!"

Spider Kane rustled about the brush for a moment. Then there was silence.

"Spy?" called Rosie.

The grass moved again. Then Spider Kane appeared. As he limped slowly back toward the others, there was a look of amazement on his face. "I don't believe it," he said to himself.

"What, Spy?" said Rosie. "Did you see someone?"

"No, Rosie, I didn't see a soul. But I did hear a cough," he said with an odd smile.

Spider Kane rummaged in the pocket of his coat and pulled out a piece of paper. He placed the paper over the letters scratched under the May-apple and carefully traced them. Then after studying the message, he whispered, "Ah, now I understand."

"Understand what?" said Leon. "What, Mr. Kane?"

It was a long moment before Spider Kane looked up from the paper. And when he did, his face was filled with dismay. "Everything. Everything, Leon," he said quietly. "I'm afraid, my friend, we have a disaster on our hands."

Spider Kane crumpled the paper and tossed it onto the ground. Then he turned up the collar of his coat and said, "I've been a fool. I must leave you now."

"Where're you going?" cried Leon.

"I'm going to visit a very old comrade."

"Who? Why? What's going on?" said Leon.

"I will explain everything later, Leon. Right now, go home with Rosie and Little Pickles."

"Tell us now!" said Leon.

"No, no," said Spider Kane. "Not until I hold cold facts in my hands, rather than mere suspicions." And with that, he turned and limped away.

❧ NINE ❧

"This will cheer us up," said Little Pickles as she pulled a tray of sweet potato scones from her clay oven.

"Not me. I can't eat," said Leon. "My stomach's too nervous." He chewed the end of his pencil as he hovered over the paper on which Spider Kane had copied the mysterious message:

HE   R MOTH ENDS THE D

"Let's see," he muttered. "The only word we can read is MOTH. But what does that mean? MOTH." He stared at Little Pickles as she served the scones with cherry jam. "What moth? Do you know any moths?"

"Lucinda Moth taught me in the first grade," said Little Pickles. "How about scones with pumpkin butter?"

"No thanks."

"Leafy, let's give this up for now," pleaded Rosie. "Wait till Spy gets back."

"Wait? I can't wait. Every minute's important. Let me see…I still think HE might be part of the word *help*."

"But so many words begin with HE," said Little Pickles. *"Heart, heck, heehaw —"*

"No, I think Mimi must have written *help* when she realized she was about to be attacked," said Leon. "And D—I have my suspicions about D."

"Oh, tons of words start with D, Leafy," said Rosie.

"Doughnuts, dumplings, doodad," said Little Pickles.

"No, no, none of them. It's *Dogtick*," growled Leon.

"Oh, c'mon, Leafy, let's not start that again," said Rosie.

"Why not?" said Leon. "Just consider it for a moment. ENDS—that probably just means *ends*. Wait a minute, wait a minute. If we try the words *help* and *Dogtick*, what do we have?" He scribbled beneath the letters:

HELP!   R MOTH ENDS THE DOGTICK

"Ah! Look!" he said, holding up the paper.

"That doesn't make a bit of sense," said Rosie. "Why don't we try leaving Dogtick out of it?"

"Wait, wait, wait," Leon said. He closed his eyes and mouthed slowly, "*Mo-th, mo-th-er, moth-er!* Oh, wow." Beneath his scribbles, he added another line. "Now, what if ENDS were *sends?*" he muttered. He added another line. "And R were part of *your?*" He scribbled yet another line.

When he was through, he let out a yelp and thrust the paper at Rosie and Little Pickles. They read:

```
HE          R MOTH ENDS THE D
HELP!       R MOTH ENDS THE DOGTICK
HELP!       R MOTHER ENDS THE DOGTICK
HELP!       R MOTHER SENDS THE DOGTICK
HELP! YOUR MOTHER SENDS THE DOGTICK
```

"That's it! That's it! *Help! Your mother sends the Dogtick!*" Leon shouted. He jumped up and down, beating his wings wildly.

"Oh, you're wrong," said Rosie.

"I'm right!" shouted Leon. "My mother swore to take action! Horrible action! She got Dogtick to do her dirty work for her. That explains everything!" His wings began to hammer the air.

"Wait, wait, wait, Leafy. Wait for Spy—"

"No! I have to find my mother!" said Leon, and he zoomed out of the cottage and headed straight toward the Flowerpot District.

❧ TEN ❧

La Mère Leafwing's cracked flowerpot was abuzz with chatter as the Women's Bug Club ate their lunch around a water lily table.

"La Mère, your *soupe à la tomate* is so delightful," said Lou Salamander. "I'm ever so pleased you're a member of our club now."

"Thank you, Lou," said La Mère, glowing.

"La Mère, darling, what a beautiful dandelion wig," said Midge Appleworm. "It's just like mine—though not quite as fluffy."

"Oh, thank you, darling, but yours is the very best, of course," said La Mère. "I only wish mine were half so elegant."

"What a fascinating-looking book," said Nymph Latell, pointing to the dusty volume on La Mère's cattail divan.

"Oh, that," said La Mère. "Yes, a friend gave it to me as a gift. Along with some good news that cheered me right up."

"Ooo! What? Tell!" said the others.

"Well, as some of you may know, my son and I had a little quarrel the other day."

"Oh, yes. The gossip I've heard is that he's become infatuated with a fluttery blue creature," said Midge Appleworm, batting her eyelashes.

"Well, that's all over now," said La Mère. "That little fly-by-night has danced right out of town. I'm certain *mon fils* will be returning to his senses very soon. So, change those rumors, will you, dearies?" She laughed happily.

"Ooo la la! Where did you get that?" said Nymph Latell, pointing to a scarf hanging on La Mère's pine cone hatrack.

La Mère fluttered to the hatrack and draped the purple silk scarf around her neck. "My friend with the book gave me this also. *Très belle,* no?"

"Wait a *minute!*" said Midge Appleworm. The plump worm rose from the table and lunged for La Mère. "That is *my* silk scarf from China! Stolen from me three weeks ago! Thief! Thief!"

Before La Mère could answer, Leon burst into the flowerpot. "Why did you do it?" he shouted. "Why?"

"What?" screamed La Mère. "Do what? What?"

"Kidnap her!" he shrieked.

"And steal from me!" yelled Midge. She pointed at the book on the cattail divan. "And I'll bet you stole that, too!"

When Leon looked at the old book, he felt faint. "*Ants at War.* Oh, Mother, how could you?" he asked in a strangled voice.

"WHAT?" screamed La Mère.

"Order Dogtick to kidnap her and then steal her things."

"Kidnap who? I didn't, I didn't! I'm no kidnapper! I'm no thief!"

"Then how did you get this?" said Midge Appleworm, wapping La Mère with the purple scarf.

"I didn't steal it," sobbed La Mère. "It was a gift!"

But Midge Appleworm grabbed her pea-pod pocketbook and started for the door. "Tell it to the judge, Pupa," she said. "Come, ladies."

With that, the three members of the Women's Bug Club huffed out of La Mère's cracked geranium pot. "*Au revoir,* thief!" Nymph Latell called over her shoulder.

"I don't understand!" La Mère cried. "I don't understand any of this."

"Mother," said Leon coldly. "Just tell me. Where is she?"

"I don't know what you're talking about, Leon! I'm innocent! I'm innocent of everything!"

"Where is she?" he shouted. "Where?"

"Excuse me for interrupting, Leon," said a deep, velvety voice. "But I do believe your mother is telling the truth."

And with that, Spider Kane crawled into the cracked clay pot, with Rosie and Little Pickles right behind.

❧ ELEVEN ❧

"Who...who are you?" sobbed La Mère.

Spider Kane took off his fedora. "My name is Spider Kane, ma'am. Sit and calm yourself."

"My mother did it, Mr. Kane. I have proof now," said Leon.

"I didn't do anything!" cried La Mère.

"There, there," said Spider Kane. "Calm down, everyone."

"Perhaps you're not aware, Mr. Kane, my

mother has *this* in her possession," said Leon. "And *this*." He held up Mimi's scarf and book. "See? Proof she's guilty."

"I'm not guilty! Those were gifts from a friend."

"Indeed they were," said Spider Kane. "Gifts from one who cares for you—and wishes you would be his friend again, no?"

"How did you know Walter Dogtick gave me those things?" asked La Mère, stunned.

"I had no difficulty recognizing the tick tracks around Mimi's residence," said Spider Kane. "But I can assure you—all of you—that Walter Dogtick did not harm the butterfly. And technically he did not steal from her, either. The poor fellow arrived on the scene after she'd disappeared and took only what he thought she'd left behind to be discarded."

"But, Mr. Kane," said Leon. "I figured out what the message under the May-apple says— *Help! Your mother sends the Dogtick.* Mimi must have scratched it in the dirt when she realized Dogtick was about to break into her home."

Spider Kane smiled. "Good work, son. But

I'm afraid you're completely wrong. The message means something else entirely."

"Really? What, Spy?" said Rosie.

"I'll share my conclusions this evening at eight o'clock. You are all invited to my home." Spider Kane turned up the collar of his coat and prepared to leave. "Oh—" he said to La Mère. "I shall also invite Walter Dogtick, ma'am. And Colonel and Mrs. Appleworm. We'll prove your innocence, once and for all. *Oui?*"

"*Merci,* Mr. Kane," La Mère said tearfully. "*Merci.*"

ᴥ TWELVE ᴥ

As the guests arrived at the elegant chambers of Spider Kane, they found him seated before a pale green leaf screen, playing his clarinet. Beside him was a mushroom table on which sat the copy of *Ants at War* and the purple silk scarf. Bean-pod chairs were placed in a semicircle with name cards on them.

As Spider Kane's soulful blues tune echoed

through his stone chambers, the guests stumbled about, locating their seats. "What is this? Symphony Hall?" grumbled Colonel Appleworm, lowering his rotund body onto a bean pod.

"Hush," said Midge Appleworm.

Only when Spider Kane had concluded his mournful song did he look at the group. "Good evening," he said slowly. Then in the soft, flickering candlelight, his gaze traveled from Leon to Rosie, to Little Pickles, to Colonel Appleworm, to Midge Appleworm, to La Mère, and finally to Walter Dogtick.

"Thank you all for coming," he said. "Let's begin." He put down his clarinet, then picked up the purple scarf from the exhibit table. "First, the mystery of the silk scarf. When did your scarf disappear, Mrs. Appleworm?"

"It was stolen three weeks ago while we were sleeping one night. It's a very expensive piece of silk made by the Wang Worms of China."

"A very expensive piece of silk made by the Wang Worms of China," said Dogtick mockingly.

La Mère snickered.

"Now see here!" said Colonel Appleworm, turning to Dogtick.

"Come, come, let's act like grownups," said Spider Kane. "Mrs. Appleworm, was the burglar who broke into your flowerpot ever caught?"

"Not until now." Midge glared at La Mère.

"Oh, go blow your nose," said La Mère.

Dogtick laughed loudly and winked at La Mère. Leon was surprised to see his mother wink back.

"Thank you, Mrs. Appleworm," said Spider Kane. "We'll let the mystery of the scarf rest for the time being. Now I'd like to introduce our first guest of the evening. Doctor Ant?"

From behind the leaf screen stepped the largest black carpenter ant Leon had ever seen. The enormous ant wore a stocking cap, a huge overcoat, and Italian lace-up shoes. On his back was a large hump.

"Allow me to introduce Dr. T. K. Ant, head librarian of the National Ant Archives," said Spider Kane. "Dr. Ant recently sought my services for another investigation. Doctor, could you please describe the incident that occurred at the Ant Archives one month before the Appleworm robbery?"

The ant cleared his throat, then spoke in a tiny falsetto. "One night, while the workers at the National Ant Archives slept, our rare-book room was robbed of three priceless manuscripts."

Spider Kane picked up Mimi's copy of *Ants at War* from the exhibit table. "Is this one of your missing manuscripts, Doctor?"

"Indeed it is."

Leon groaned. But Spider Kane did not look at him. "Thank you, Doctor."

Dr. Ant took a little bow and went back behind the screen.

"Now I'd like to introduce a bee who recently sought my services," said Spider Kane. "General?"

No one appeared.

"General?" said Spider Kane.

"Be right there," someone hummed.

A moment later, from behind the leaf screen

stepped a portly bumblebee shrouded in a bright blue cape with a blue soldier cap pulled down around his ears. Leon noticed that oddly enough the bee was also wearing Italian lace-up shoes—just like the ones worn by Dr. T. K. Ant.

"Who's this clown?" mumbled Colonel Appleworm.

"Hush," said Midge as she and the others leaned forward, spellbound.

"I'd like to introduce Major General Robert Bum, steward of the queen and deputy treasurer of Bee City," said Spider Kane. "Bob, did a burglary also occur this spring in Bee City? A robbery of the worst kind?"

"Mmm-hmm," said Major General Bum.

"The Queen Bee's diamond crown was stolen. Correct?" said Spider Kane.

"Mmm-hmm."

Leon groaned again and covered his face.

"A crown matching the description I gave you of the one Leon saw at Mimi's?" said Spider Kane.

"Mmm-hmm. Mmm-hmm." Major General

Bum dropped his head and hummed sorrowfully. "Hmmmmmmmmmmmmmmmmmmmmmmm."

"Thank you, Bob," said Spider Kane.

"Hmmmmmmmmmmmmmmmmmmmmmmmmm-mmmmmmmmmmmmmmmmm."

"Thank you, Bob!"

Major General Bum shook himself, then buzzed back behind the leaf screen.

The group broke into excited murmuring.

"Gracious," said Little Pickles. "I think I'm beginning to see the light."

"Yes," said Spider Kane. "I imagine all of you are groping toward the same conclusion."

"No, no," Leon moaned.

"*She* stole all those things, didn't she, Mr. Kane?" shouted La Mère triumphantly. "That tacky Mimi! What did I tell you, Leon—your friend was a desperate thief."

"Indeed, Mimi was desperate, ma'am," said Spider Kane. "Not many of us would risk our lives to mend the mischief done by others."

"What do you mean, Spy?" said Rosie.

"Mimi was not a thief. She was only trying to

return the stolen items to their rightful owners."

"Oh, whaddya mean?" said Dogtick.

"If you had not trampled the message scratched in the dirt under the May-apple, Mr. Dogtick, we might have spared you and Mrs. Leafwing a great deal of embarrassment."

Spider Kane tacked a large piece of paper to his leaf screen and wrote:

HE   R MOTH ENDS THE D

"I'm afraid this does not mean *Help! Your mother sends the Dogtick*, Leon. If you study it a bit more, you'll see there's not enough room between MOTH and ENDS to add E, R, and S."

"Oh, you're right. I'm an idiot," said Leon.

"It was a good try, my friend. And I wish for Mimi's sake you'd been right. For the real message, I'm afraid, is utterly horrifying."

Spider Kane turned back to the paper and slowly filled in the missing letters. When he stepped aside, the group read:

THE EMPEROR MOTH ENDS THE DAY

"The message under the May-apple was not a cry for help from Mimi," Spider Kane said softly. "It was the arrogant boasting of an insane moth."

❧ THIRTEEN ❧

As Spider Kane lit his pipe, murmurs of confusion rippled through the crowd.

"What do you mean, Mr. Kane?" cried Leon.

"The Emperor Moth has kidnapped Mimi," said Spider Kane.

"But who is he? Who's the Emperor Moth?"

"Allow me to introduce one who can answer that far better than I." Spider Kane stepped behind the leaf screen and a moment later ushered out one of the strangest-looking moths Leon had ever seen.

Oddly enough, the moth wore the same Italian lace-up shoes as Dr. Ant and General Bum. But the rest of his clothing was considerably shabbier. He had a soiled red bandanna tied around his head and a black patch over one eye.

His other eye twitched as a creepy smile cracked his face.

But suddenly a deep, racking cough wiped the smile away. It was the same cough Leon had heard behind the rosemary hedge and near the May-apple.

"Is dat the Emperor guy?" asked Dogtick.

"No, Mr. Dogtick. This is a former aide to the Emperor Moth—Sergeant Thomas Hawkins, better known as 'the Hawk.'"

"Oh, my gosh!" said Rosie.

The Hawk threw her a little salute.

"He's the one I told you about, sonny!" La Mère shouted. "The one I saw with that Mimi. They were embracing by the Lily Pond."

Jerking around to face La Mère, the Hawk fixed his eye on her and in a rasping, whispery voice said, "And what business is that of yours, madame?"

At the sound of the Hawk's voice, La Mère fluttered back in fright. Leon shivered. The Hawk had the voice of one who'd lived under a rock far too long.

"The Hawk, Rosie, and I all served together during the Mosquito Wars," said Spider Kane. "We were good friends until the Hawk became a hired soldier for the Emperor Moth."

"Why did you go work for him, Hawk?" said Rosie.

The Hawk smiled bitterly, then rasped, "I always preferred night work, Rosie. By the time I realized that night work with the Emperor meant crime and deceit, it was too late. By then I'd burrowed too deep into the dark."

"I hadn't seen the Hawk for ages," said Spider Kane. "But this morning, when I heard a deep cough near the May-apple, a shock of recognition went through me. It was the same dry hack that used to keep me awake nights in our tent. So I followed the retreating cough through the Wildflower Woods—until I found the Hawk hiding under a cold rock."

The moth nodded at Spider Kane. "And it's good to be with you again, Cap'n. And you too, Lieutenant Rose."

"Now, will you kindly tell us, Hawk, about

the Emperor Moth?" said Spider Kane.

"The Emperor Moth is the emperor of the Dark Swamp," the Hawk rasped. "His island palace is no more than the rotting stump of a black ash. In spite of his riches, he chooses to live in wood rot and decay."

"How awful," said Little Pickles.

The Hawk shot a look at her. His eye burned with a horrid intensity. "He loves black, spongy earth, my lady. He loves leaf mold and fungus. He loves damp soil crawling with worms. He loves robber-flies and beetle grubs. He *loves* the underbelly of life."

"This goon's making me sick," said Colonel Appleworm.

The Hawk whirled around to face the colonel. "Yes, Colonel. I *was* a goon." He leaned forward menacingly. "I was the goon who silently crept into your flowerpot one dark night and stole your dear wife's precious purple scarf."

"Horrors!" said Midge. "Mr. Kane, you mean *this* creature was prowling about our home while Tubby and I slept?"

Colonel Appleworm pinched his wife for using his private nickname in public.

The Hawk threw back his head and laughed grotesquely. "Yes," he rasped, "yes, I was the goon who did it! I was the goon who crept about on tippytoes while you and Tubby slept. I was the goon who heard Tubby snoring as I plucked the scarf out of your fancy cedar-chip closet! I was the goon—"

"Ease up, Hawk," said Spider Kane.

"Sorry, Cap'n. Sorry." The Hawk pulled in his wings and bowed his head.

"I still don't understand. Why did you do these things, Hawk?" asked Rosie.

"Because I was a fool, Lieutenant Rose," said the Hawk in a hoarse and muffled voice. "I grew confused about the difference between right and wrong, and I did whatever the emperor ordered."

"Why did he order you to steal?"

The Hawk looked at Rosie. "Because the Emperor Moth loves to end each day with a crime. At dusk, he dresses in his maroon velvet suit and his white gloves. Then he gives his goons their orders for the evening. We go out and plunder the Ant Kingdom and Bee City—and the Flowerpot District of the well-to-do."

"Does the emperor himself go with you, Hawk?"

"Ha!" An angry smile crossed the Hawk's face. "The emperor seldom leaves the palace. But when he does, he always leaves his calling card at the scene of the crime—*The Emperor Moth Ends the Day.*"

"The message that was left near Mimi's burrow under the May-apple," Spider Kane said.

"But, Mr. Kane!" cried Leon. "How come the emperor gave Mimi the stuff he stole? And why did he kidnap her?"

Spider Kane looked at Leon with sad and somber eyes. "Because, Leon, your friend Mimi is the Emperor Moth's wife—the Empress of the Dark Swamp."

With a tiny groan, Leon fainted.

FOURTEEN

"Drink this, sweetie." Little Pickles gave Leon some water as the rest of the group whispered excitedly. Then Spider Kane helped him back into his seat.

"See, sonny!" said La Mère. "She wasn't only tacky, she was wicked!"

"Mrs. Leafwing," said Spider Kane. "I suggest you hold your judgments until you hear from my final guest."

As Spider Kane again stepped behind the pale leaf screen, Colonel Appleworm laughed out loud. "How in the world do they all fit back there, Midge?"

"Hush," said his wife.

A moment later, Spider Kane returned with a feeble gossamer-winged butterfly leaning on his arm. Leon gave a start—the butterfly looked just like Mimi! She had beautiful blue iridescent wings just like Mimi's. And her face was just like Mimi's, except for its deep, sad wrinkles.

"Perhaps Mimi's mother can help us understand," Spider Kane said. "Margaret?"

"One summer day a year ago, my daughter and I were in the woods sniffing flowers," the old butterfly began in a nasal, monotone voice. "Before I knew it, she was flitting away from me, looking for daffodils.

"As soon as she was out of my sight, I heard screaming. I flew as fast as I could. But when I came to a clearing, I saw a great winged creature flying into the air, carrying away my precious child. Her screams—still—echo—in my ears...."

As the old butterfly hid her face and shook with sobs, Leon heard loud weeping elsewhere in the room. He turned and saw his mother waving her handkerchief dramatically. "Oh, that poor, poor mother!" she wailed.

"Empress Mimi was forced to share the Worm Wood Throne in the Hall of Decay, and she practically died of grief," rasped the Hawk.

La Mère sobbed louder. Dogtick patted her on the back sympathetically. "That poor, poor mother," repeated La Mère.

"Over time, as Mimi sat in the dimly lit, damp throne room, she nearly forgot her life in the sun," said the Hawk. "She grew thin and weak.

But she always stayed kind. She smiled at me when I hadn't seen a smile in a long, long time." The Hawk looked away and took a deep breath. "So! I decided to help her escape. It was the first decent thing I'd done since I fought for Cap'n Kane."

Spider Kane nodded encouragingly. "Go on, Hawk," he said.

"Before Mimi went back to her mother, she wanted to return some of the emperor's stolen goods," said the Hawk. "So I brought her here to the Cottage Garden. After we hugged good-bye near the Lily Pond, I kept watch over her. Only"—the Hawk rolled his head back in anguish—"only I was sleeping when that monster came and—and—and caught—her—" The Hawk fell on the floor, convulsed with rage.

"But how did the emperor know where she was?" cried Leon.

Spider Kane stepped forward. "It seems that Mimi's first mission—returning the silk scarf to Mrs. Appleworm—was interrupted by the good intentions of a kind stranger, Leon. *You*. Soon the whole Garden was gossiping about your interest in her. The gossip spread until it reached the emperor himself."

"Argh!" Leon cried out. "It was *my* fault!" He fell beside the Hawk and beat his fists against the floor.

"Spy, do you think the emperor killed her?" said Rosie.

"No, Lieutenant Rose, I sincerely don't. My hunch is he expects Mimi to be his empress again. I imagine he enjoys forcing her to rule the Island of the Dark Swamp against her will. Only this time, I'm sure she's very well guarded."

"We must save her, then!" cried Leon.

"Yeah, Cap'n!" croaked the Hawk.

"And help that poor mother!" wailed La Mère.

Spider Kane smiled. "I'm so glad we all agree, my friends. I've been quite restless since the Mosquito Wars ended."

PART III

✀ FIFTEEN ✀

"Mom?" said Leon, peeking into his mother's cracked geranium pot.

La Mère was packing her things, and Walter Dogtick was helping her. "You want to take this, Pupa?" Walter said, holding up her dandelion wig.

"Yep. Pack it up, lamb chop. It'll be good for a laugh someday," said La Mère.

Walter carefully put the dandelion wig into his old soiled sack.

"Mom?" said Leon. "What's going on?"

"I'm hittin' the road, sonny," said La Mère as she snapped a cheap strand of pop beads around her neck. "Those snobs at the Women's Bug Club won't have La Mère Leafwing to kick around anymore!"

"Where're you going?" said Leon.

"Back to the ole Goatweed Patch."

"Goatweed Patch?"

"Yep. I'm gonna take up residence in the empty chamber of an old wasp nest."

"But you always hated the Goatweed Patch," said Leon.

"Well, perhaps I don't hate it so much anymore, buster. At least the little buggies who live there don't go around with their noses stuck up in the air. And they don't run around falsely accusing one another, either." La Mère's lip trembled. Dogtick placed a comforting hand on her back. "And life must go on, huh, Wally?" she said.

"Dat's right, precious."

"And at least I have you."

"Dat's right, precious," said the old tick.

"So you two are good friends again?" said Leon.

La Mère grinned fondly at Dogtick. "The *best*," she said.

"I'm glad," Leon said, and he meant it.

Dogtick sighed. "Don't never say true love don't win out," he said to Leon.

"I hope you're right."

"You really care for that little butterfly, don't you, sonny?" said La Mère.

Leon nodded sadly.

"Well, I hope she turns up—for her mother's sake, of course. When do you characters leave on your little expedition?"

"At sundown we're meeting Spider Kane at the edge of the Garden," said Leon. "We'll sleep under the Honeysuckle Arch, then leave for the Dark Swamp and the emperor's island."

"Oh." La Mère stared at Leon as if she'd only just now become aware of the danger he was heading into. "Oh, honey," she gasped. "Don't let that ugly emperor grab you."

Leon laughed a little. "I won't, don't worry."

"I want you safe and—and happy, baby. Like what any good mother wants for her son."

"I know, I know," said Leon. He leaned over and kissed her. "I'm sorry I wrongly accused you," he whispered.

La Mère's eyes flooded with tears, and she sniffed. "Well, *you* I'll forgive. But not those horrible ex-friends of mine!" She let out a deep sob, then waved away her tears with a wing flutter and held her head up proudly. "Ready?" she said to Dogtick.

The grubby old tick nodded.

"Then climb on, lamb chop," she said.

Walter Dogtick climbed on La Mère's back, clutching his dirty sack to his chest.

"Good-bye, sonny!" La Mère called to Leon. "Tell that nasty emperor I'll kill him if he lays a hand on you!"

"Okay," said Leon, smiling.

La Mère threw him a kiss. Then she fluttered out of her cracked pot and carried Walter Dogtick away into the bright blue summer sky.

❧ SIXTEEN ❧

That evening when Leon arrived at the edge of the Garden, he found the others sitting around a small campfire, eating a dinner of crusty bread and roasted potatoes. Spider Kane, Rosie, Little Pickles, and the Hawk all looked quite amazing in the glow of the firelight.

Spider Kane wore his dark blue captain's uniform with a white glove on every hand, and he carried a canvas rucksack. Rosie wore her khaki-colored uniform. Little Pickles wore her reserve army uniform and carried a wicker picnic basket. And the Hawk wore a tattered gray jacket covered with tarnished medals.

Though they all greeted him warmly and offered him dinner, Leon felt very young and inexperienced next to them. He wore his bright green Bug Scout uniform, but it was too small. He tugged on his sleeves as he sat silently in the shadows and listened to the others plan the rescue mission.

"We'll get a good night's sleep here under the Honeysuckle Arch," said Spider Kane. He lit his pipe, then added, "At dawn, we'll move out of the Garden and head into the Forest."

"What route will we take, Spy?" asked Rosie.

"I've made a map," said Spider Kane. He reached into his rucksack, pulled out a tiny scrap of paper, and spread it on the ground in front of them.

Spider Kane traced their path with a white-gloved finger. "The Forest, the Dark Swamp, the emperor's island. We'll arrive at the Swamp by nightfall, then make our way to the palace in the dark."

When the last light had faded from the sky, Spider Kane ordered them to turn in. "We have a long day ahead of us."

"Right, Cap'n," rasped the Hawk. "A long day—and night."

Spider Kane kept watch beside the fire while the others nestled down to sleep. Rosie and Little Pickles lay on small mats of woven grass, and the Hawk held his wings rooflike over his back.

As Leon looked up at the stars, he inhaled the sweet scent of the honeysuckle. He listened to Spider Kane tap his pipe against a log. He listened to peepers and bullfrogs calling from the Lily Pond. Just as he started to sink into sleep, a deep growling noise made him jump with fear. "What's that?" he cried.

Spider Kane chuckled. "Just the Hawk snoring," he said.

"Gracious," said Little Pickles.

Leon snuggled deeper into the grass and closed his eyes again. Suddenly the shrill cry of an unknown creature echoed in the distance. "What's that?" he said.

"It's the world outside the Garden, Leon," said Spider Kane in his deep, velvety voice.

Never in his life had Leon ventured outside the Cottage Garden. Suddenly the world on the other side of the stone wall seemed infinitely large and dangerous.

Leon lay down again and squeezed his eyes shut. As the wind rustled through the grass and weeds, he thought he heard whispers that said, *The Emperor Moth ends the day.*

Shivering in the damp darkness, Leon longed for warmth and daylight. He longed to see Mimi again. But the whisperings swelled in the breeze, saying, *The night is here to stay.*

SEVENTEEN

Leon woke just before dawn. The scent of chicory weed tea wafted through the air as gray light was beginning to filter through the lacy leaves overhead. As he stared up at the sky, he heard Spider Kane's voice: "I like what I've seen so far," the spider said.

"I don't know, Spy," someone answered. It was a male voice Leon had never heard before. It was smooth and clear, nothing like the Hawk's rasping, throaty growl. "I still think he's too young. We wouldn't want anything to happen to a kid."

Leon jerked completely awake. Who was talking? And were they talking about him? He scrambled off the ground and flitted through the haze until he came upon the Hawk, Spider Kane, Rosie, and Little Pickles sitting near the campfire, sipping tea from acorn caps.

He quickly darted over to them. "Good morning," he said.

The Hawk cleared his throat and rasped,

"Mornin', kid."

"Who was just here? I heard a strange voice," Leon said.

"Just us," said Rosie.

"Want some chicory weed tea, sweetie?" said Little Pickles.

Leon was confused. But at the moment he was more disturbed about *what* he had heard than about *who* had said it. Had they all been debating whether or not to take him along?

"Sure, I'll have some tea," said Leon. Actually he hated the bitter-tasting stuff. But this morning he'd force himself to drink it.

As Little Pickles poured more tea from a stone pot into an acorn cap, Spider Kane gave Leon a reassuring smile. "How'd you sleep?" he asked.

"Never better in my life," said Leon, though in fact he'd hardly slept at all.

"Good. Because today's probably going to be the longest day in your life," said Spider Kane.

"I've had longer," said Leon.

The spider nodded kindly, and Leon felt a bit

ashamed for acting so defensive.

"Here you go, kid," the Hawk said as he passed the acorn cap.

"Leon. My name is Leon," said Leon.

"Good name," rasped the Hawk, giving him a crooked smile.

"When we start out, the Hawk and I will lead the way," said Spider Kane. "Then Rosie, then Little Pickles, and then Leon."

"I'm at the very end?" piped Leon before he could stop himself.

Spider Kane nodded. "I need you to guard against a rear attack."

Leon gulped. "Rear attack?"

"Hey, Cap'n, maybe you should give that job to Lieutenant Rose," said the Hawk.

"No, I want it," said Leon.

"This ain't no Bug Scouts, you know, Leon," rasped the Hawk. "It's a dangerous mission."

"I know that. I was the one who wanted to rescue Mimi in the first place, remember?"

"Calm down, Leon," said Spider Kane. "I think the Hawk is just worried that the emperor's henchmen may be patrolling the Forest."

"Yeah, his robber-flies," said the Hawk, "his assassin bugs, his mosquito commandos, his grubs, his—"

"Okay, honey," said Rosie. "We get the picture."

"Then, if there're no more questions, let's be off," said Spider Kane.

The little army moved out of the Garden and into the Forest, Spider Kane crawling with his slight limp alongside the low-flying Hawk. Behind him, Rosie and Little Pickles bumped through the air. Leon brought up the rear.

As he fluttered through the new world of the Forest, Leon's eyes darted from creeping vines and peeling bark to blackened roots and moss-covered rocks. Winding in and out among spindly saplings and furrowed gray tree trunks, he was terrified of caws and rustlings coming from the shadows.

Then, to his horror, a damp fog began to roll through the Forest. Soon all the trees and brush were blanketed in a thick white cloud.

Clickity click, click.

Leon looked about anxiously. The clicking noise was unlike other Forest sounds. But in the fog he couldn't see where it was coming from.

Clickity click, click.

Leon almost cried out for help, but he stopped himself. It was his job to protect the army from a rear attack.

Click, clickity click.

The clicking seemed to be coming from farther back in the Forest. Leon fluttered toward it, then stopped and waited.

The noise did not come again.

As Leon hovered in the ghostly vapor, he felt as if he were being watched by unseen eyes. The Forest seemed strangely still, and the air felt cold and clammy. He shivered, then turned and began hurrying back to find the others.

But Leon was lost. He couldn't find his friends in the fog. "Rosie! Little Pickles! Mr. Kane!" he cried. He was certain something was following him. As he tried to escape, he flew into sticky webs and grasping vines. He banged into trees and fallen limbs. Battered and bruised, he screamed, "Help! Help!"

Just when Leon thought he was going to die of terror, four white-gloved hands reached out of the gloom.

Leon beat his wings frantically as Spider Kane grabbed him.

"Be still," the spider said, holding him tightly. "Be still."

❧ EIGHTEEN ❧

"Fear is a trickster, Leon," said Spider Kane. "You must banish him before he tricks you into a panic. Only then can you solve the problem at hand."

Leon was still so frightened he could barely speak.

"How'd you lose us, Leafy?" said Rosie.

"I thought I heard something behind me," Leon mumbled, "so I went to check on it."

"What did it sound like?" asked Spider Kane.

"It was some sort of clicking noise."

"*Clicking* noise?" Spider Kane ran a hand over his face.

The Hawk groaned. "Are you thinkin' what I'm thinkin', Cap'n?"

Spider Kane nodded silently.

"What are you thinking?" cried Leon.

"Deathwatch beetles," whispered Spider Kane.

Leon stopped breathing.

"Tapping a telegraph message to the emperor," rasped the Hawk. "Telling him about us."

"Oh, no!" Leon burst into tears. He couldn't help himself.

"Oh, don't cry, Leon," pleaded Little Pickles. "Everything's okay. It's not what you think! We're all just—"

"Little Pickles!" interrupted Rosie. "What are you saying?"

"We're all just—what?" cried Leon.

Little Pickles looked as if she'd suddenly swallowed a gnat. "I—I just meant that things usually work out for the best, don't they, Rosie?"

"Sure they do," said Rosie. Then she turned

to Leon. "Are you all right, Leafy?"

"Yes, yes, I'm fine," Leon gasped as he dried his eyes on his Bug Scout sleeve. "I'm sorry. I just—I just lost control…"

"It happens to all of us, Leon," said Spider Kane kindly. "Come on, let's get—"

"Wait! Shhh!" said the Hawk. "Listen!"

Leon's heart caught in his throat as he listened to an eerie whining sound coming from the distance. He couldn't see through the fog, but the noise was growing louder and louder.

"Aw, nuts!" said the Hawk.

"Mosquito patrol!" said Spider Kane. "Hide! Hide!"

They all scattered into the mist. Leon, Rosie, and Little Pickles scooted into a curled brown oak leaf. As the whining noise grew louder and louder, Leon trembled inside the musty-smelling tunnel and whispered to his pounding heart, "Be still, be still."

Finally the terrible sound faded away.

When they heard the Hawk coughing, Leon, Rosie, and Little Pickles crept slowly out of the curled leaf.

"They'll be back," said Spider Kane. "They won't give up. Let's move, *fast*."

The fog began to lift as Leon fluttered quickly behind Rosie and Little Pickles. Still he jumped at every sound—at every cough of the Hawk, every *snap* of a breaking twig, every *chur* of a snowy tree cricket.

Several times he hit the ground and held his breath when the terrible wing whine of the mosquitoes sounded from the distance. But each time, the whirring patrol moved on.

Finally in the late afternoon the little army left the Forest and began climbing a weedy slope at the edge of the Dark Swamp. The weeds were so thick and high that Leon could barely see his friends as they preceded him up the hill. But suddenly he heard Spider Kane utter, "Good heavens!"

Leon zoomed to the crest of the hill. Squeezing between Rosie and Little Pickles, he peered down at the shore and saw a sight he would not forget for the rest of his life.

NINETEEN

A huge, wriggling mass was moving across the sandbank of the Dark Swamp.

"How awful!" breathed Little Pickles.

"What are they doing, Spy?" said Rosie.

"Military exercises," said Spider Kane.

For the first time, Leon realized the writhing mass was a horde of grubs. He couldn't speak or move as he stared at the hideous army parading up and down the sandbank.

"We'll never get past them alive, Spy," said Rosie.

"She's right, Cap'n," said the Hawk.

Spider Kane turned to Leon. "What do you think?" he said.

Leon was shocked that Spider Kane even cared what he thought. "Um, I think we can do it," he said, trying to sound brave.

"Ah, kid, you don't know these guys," rasped the Hawk.

But Spider Kane kept staring at Leon. "Tell us, son," he said. "How do you think we can get past them to rescue Mimi?"

Mimi. Just the sound of her name made Leon ache. He would do anything to save her. "Maybe we can fly," he said.

"That's fine for you and me, kid," said the Hawk. "But the ladybugs are a bit slow and the Cap'n's earthbound."

"Well, what if you carry Rosie and Little Pickles? And I'll carry Mr. Kane," said Leon.

"Nah, kid, he's twice your size," said the Hawk.

"Maybe I can hang from you by one of my cobweb threads, Leon," said Spider Kane. "You want to try it?"

"Yes, sir."

"Good." Spider Kane took a ball of cobweb from his rucksack. He snipped off a short filament and lashed the end of it to Leon's Bug Scout sash.

"There," he said. "Now, Rosie, Little Pickles, climb on the Hawk's back." When they were ready to go, Spider Kane saluted them. Then the Hawk took off into the twilight, carrying the two ladybugs.

"All right, Leon," said Spider Kane. "Follow the Hawk and fly as high and swiftly as you can."

As Leon lifted off the ground, Spider Kane swung beneath him like a kite in the wind. Leon rocked from side to side and almost flipped over. But he steadied himself, then fluttered higher and higher after the Hawk—until he and Spider Kane sailed unnoticed over the emperor's wretched army.

Then, suddenly, the most extraordinary thing happened. Leon thought he saw Mimi in the distance. She was fluttering toward the emperor's island, her blue wings shining in the fleeting gray light.

Was his fear playing another trick on him? "MIMI!" he screamed. And in the twilight, from far away, the mysterious vision seemed to turn and look at him with an expression of utter horror.

Suddenly Spider Kane jerked so hard on his cobweb thread that Leon somersaulted through the air. When he finally steadied himself again, night had cloaked the stream in darkness, and his vision of Mimi had vanished.

❧ TWENTY ❧

"It looked just like her," Leon was explaining to the group as they huddled together in the marsh grass at the edge of the island.

"Sometimes in the twilight our deepest dreams and wishes shimmer before our eyes," said Spider Kane. "But what you saw, Leon, was not a gossamer-winged butterfly. It was a violet damselfly. I saw her too."

"Are you sure? Maybe Mimi escaped from the emperor's palace," said Leon.

"Look! There it is," said the Hawk.

The moon was peeking out from behind a cloud. And now in the dim light, the group could see the silhouette of the rotting stump of a black ash.

"That's where Mimi really is, Leon," whispered Spider Kane.

As Leon stared at the monstrous palace, his vision of Mimi faded into the gloom. He felt sick now, imagining her trapped inside the black stump.

"During the night, the blue lamps of glow-worms light the winding corridors," the Hawk said in a terrible whisper. "One passageway leads to the Hall of Decay. Another to a dungeon filled with the claws and wings of the traitors the emperor has starved to death."

"Oh, my," said Little Pickles. "What wickedness."

"Yes, and wickedness longs to entwine itself with goodness, Little Pickles," said Spider Kane. "That's why the emperor wants to keep Mimi as his queen."

"I don't care why he wants to keep her. We've got to save her!" said Leon.

"Cool down, kid," rasped the Hawk. "Or you'll be joining those bug parts in the dungeon."

"This is the plan," said Spider Kane. "I want the three of you to wait here while the Hawk and I head into the palace."

"Can't I go with you?" asked Leon.

"Don't worry, Leon. We need your help, but later," said Spider Kane. "First we have to split into two regiments. The Hawk is going to guide me through a secret tunnel that leads to the royal chambers where the emperor and Mimi sleep.

"As we travel through the palace, I'll spin a thread for the three of you. Once we're safely hiding inside an empty gallery, I'll tug on the thread. Follow it. When you join us, we'll rescue Mimi together."

"But what if his guards see your thread? This won't work! What if they capture you? I don't understand," said Leon.

"Oh, Leafy, soon it will all make sense," said Little Pickles.

"Let's just do what Spy says," said Rosie.

"Trust me, Leon," said Spider Kane. He reached into his rucksack and took out his ball of cobweb thread. Then he handed Leon the end. "When you feel a strong tug, follow the thread to the palace."

"C'mon, Cap'n, we can go now!" said the Hawk. "The blue lamps are comin' on. They'll be heading for bed."

"Wait," said Leon. "I still don't understand. What if—"

"Be brave," whispered Spider Kane to him.

Then he and the Hawk crept away into the night.

"But what if they get caught?" Leon said.

"During the Mosquito Wars, Spy captured whole armies by throwing cobweb nets over them," whispered Rosie. "And the Hawk can do anything."

"What do you mean—'do anything'?" said Leon.

"Oh, I just mean he seems to be quite clever," said Little Pickles.

A memory of the early morning came back to Leon. "When I woke up," he said, "I heard a voice that didn't sound like the Hawk or Spider Kane. Who was talking?"

"Oh, I have no idea, Leafy," said Rosie. "The morning seems a million years away."

"Yes, it's all quite a blur to me," said Little Pickles.

Clouds scudded across the moon, and the wind moaned. As Leon stared in silence at the dark palace, he felt very alone. For some reason, he no longer completely trusted Rosie and Little

Pickles. Everyone in the group seemed to know things he didn't.

Suddenly Leon felt a tug on the thread. "Hey!" he cried. "Let's go!"

"But it's too soon!" cried Rosie.

Then the thread was jerked from Leon's hands. He yelped. "Oh, no! It's gone!"

"Gone?"

"It got yanked away! Something happened!" Suddenly all Leon wanted to do was fly home.

"Maybe Spy fell or something," said Rosie.

"Oh, no—then he's hurt," said Leon.

"No, no, I don't think so," said Rosie. "Spiders never get hurt when they fall."

Leon's mind suddenly leaped to a faraway time and place. "What falls down and never gets hurt?" he asked the night.

"What?" said Rosie.

"Snow," he answered softly, and he remembered her lovely laugh, her little song, and her dance, and he moaned with sorrow.

"Leafy? What's wrong?"

"I almost forgot her," he whispered. "Mimi."

He looked at Rosie. "I have to save Mimi, no matter what. I'm going into the palace."

"We'll go with you!" said Rosie.

"Good. Climb on my back."

Rosie and Little Pickles hoisted themselves onto Leon. Then the three of them took off through the moonless dark, headed for the emperor's palace.

✺ TWENTY-ONE ✺

The stench of decay filled the air as Leon, Rosie, and Little Pickles lit down at the base of the black ash stump.

"Where's the entrance?" whispered Leon.

"There's a blue light," said Rosie, pointing to a glowworm lamp. It was shining inside a crumbling hole that was nearly covered with peeling bark. "I'll go in there. Then you two follow me. Count to ten before you come."

"Wait," said Leon, his courage starting to leave him. "Let's stay together."

"We can't. We should go one at a time," said Rosie. "If one of us gets caught, the others can come to the rescue. I'll go first. Then Little Pickles. Then you."

"Wait, wait," whispered Leon. But before he could say anything more, Rosie crept into the stump.

"This is crazy," Leon said to Little Pickles. "We need more of a plan."

But the ladybug wasn't listening. "Eight, nine, ten," she whispered, then vanished into the stump after Rosie.

"Little Pick—!" Leon said, but it was too late. He was all alone.

Suddenly a scream came from inside the palace. It sounded like Rosie! Then another scream—Little Pickles! Then there was silence.

But the screams echoed in Leon's ears as if the very night were screaming. Unbearably afraid, he fluttered off the ground and hovered in the dark. Half of him was desperate to escape the terror inside the palace. The other half was overwhelmed with fury and determination.

The rising wind whispered, *Escape! Escape!*

But Leon said, "No!" And he darted to the entrance of the hollow stump and crept into the emperor's palace.

The blue glowworm lamps lit the walls of the palace. Numerous black tunnels spread like veins around the curved, worm-eaten walls. Leon saw no signs of anyone—not his friends, not the emperor, not the emperor's guards.

But then he heard music—clear, melancholy strains coming from a higher level in the stump. It sounded as if Spider Kane were playing his clarinet. Perhaps the emperor was forcing the spider to entertain him while his friends were being tortured.

Rage pushed Leon down the winding tunnel that led to the clarinet sounds. The music grew louder and louder as he crawled along the dank-smelling worm-eaten wood, then passed through empty galleries lit by dim blue lights.

The music stopped just as Leon fluttered into a large hollow space. It was a dead end. Looking wildly about the chamber, he still saw no signs of grub guards or robber-flies. No signs of Little

Pickles, Rosie, the Hawk, or Spider Kane. And no signs of Mimi or the Emperor Moth.

"Rosie?" he whispered frantically. "Little Pickles?"

Silence.

Leon's fear began to turn into panic. He felt close to fainting, but he clenched his fists. "No! No!" he whispered fiercely. Then he took a deep breath. And as he let the air out slowly, a calm and deadly anger banished the trickster within him. For the first time in his life, he felt absolutely sure of himself. *Emperor!* he called.

Silence.

"Emperor Moth, come out here! Where are you?" His voice now shook with rage.

"Here."

Leon jerked around as a spindly figure stepped from the shadows. "I'm here, Leon," he said.

"Mr. Kane!" cried Leon. "Where's everyone else? Where's the Emperor Moth?"

"Here," said Spider Kane. On his thin lips was a smile.

"Where?" said Leon, looking about.

"Here," said Spider Kane.

"Where?"

"*I* am the Emperor Moth," said Spider Kane.

❧ TWENTY-TWO ❧

"*You?*" said Leon.

"Yes," said Spider Kane.

"*You* are the Emperor Moth?"

"Yes."

"Wh-what do you mean?"

"Emperor Moth is my code name," said Spider Kane.

Leon stepped back. Spider Kane looked larger than before. His voice sounded deeper. And in the light of the blue lamps, his face had an expression of deadly seriousness.

"Your—your code name?" Leon felt as if he couldn't breathe.

"I'm the commander of a secret band called the Order of the MOTH, Leon."

The wind whistled eerily through the dark stump. "Wh-what's that?"

"Before I explain, allow me to introduce my most trusted lieutenants."

Out of the shadows stepped Rosie, then Little Pickles, and then the Hawk.

"What's going on?" breathed Leon.

"Now let me introduce one other lieutenant," said Spider Kane.

Mimi entered the hall, carrying a blue lamp.

Leon laughed a short, hysterical laugh. This was a dream, a crazy nightmare that was rolling over him just as the fog had rolled through the Forest earlier.

But Spider Kane looked very real in the cold blue light. "We are all members of the Order of the MOTH," he said. "Recently Rosie and Little Pickles urged me to make you a member also. They've watched you grow up. And they claimed that you were strong and dependable. I believed that you were still too young to join us. However, we all finally agreed to send you on a quest. The journey had to be very difficult. For someday, we all might have to place our lives in your hands."

"I'm sorry I couldn't tell you the truth, Leafy," said Rosie.

"I was dying to tell you," said Little Pickles.

"She almost did," said Rosie.

Leon felt dizzy. The wind blew harder than ever, and the blue lights made his head swirl.

"Allow me to introduce you to Thomas Hawkins," said Spider Kane. "The greatest living actor of the moth world."

"Welcome to the emperor's palace, Leon," said the Hawk in a smooth, soft voice. Then he pulled off his eye patch and red bandanna.

"You played your part perfectly, Hawk," said Spider Kane. "And so did you, Leon. Don't think for a moment Mimi wasn't aware that you and your mother were watching her when she dropped the scarf."

"Does—does my mother know about this?" Leon said, trembling.

"Oh, my, no. I must say her untimely threats nearly upset our whole plan. She and the innocent Mr. Dogtick stumbled into our little drama quite unexpectedly."

"And then I nearly ruined everything by getting here too late," said Mimi. "I almost died when I saw you flying over the water!"

Leon stared at Mimi. "So—so you were never the empress of the Dark Swamp?"

"No, I'm just a part-time actress Spy once directed in a production of *Bug's Delight*."

"I guess—I guess you thought I was an idiot, then," Leon stammered. He looked at Mimi with a stricken expression. "You must have had a great laugh when you told them about my fear of h-having skinny arms, and my singing, and they must have all laughed about the fact that I liked you—a lot!"

Before anyone could say anything, Leon turned and fluttered blindly away from the group. He rushed down the dank-smelling black tunnel and through the worm-eaten wood galleries. He crashed into peeling bark and crumbling walls until finally he arrived at the jagged entrance of the stump.

As he staggered outside, the cool wind and grass seemed to be laughing at him.

Leon froze at the sound of the deep, velvety voice behind him.

"You can't escape us, Leon," said Spider Kane.

"Leave me alone," said Leon, his teeth chattering. "I'm not as d-dumb as you think. I knew something was f-fishy. I heard a strange voice at the campsite, remember? And I said I saw Mimi, re-remember? I saw her, but you tried to make me think I was d-dreaming!"

"Leon, listen. This wasn't mere fun at your expense," said Spider Kane. "It was a deadly serious quest. It was the only way the Order of the MOTH could discover the answers to many important questions."

"Wh-what questions?"

Rosie's voice bounced from the cold dark: "In spite of his young age, could Leon Leafwing navigate the world outside the Cottage Garden?"

Then came Little Pickles: "If Leon Leafwing lost his leader, would he still continue the quest?"

And the Hawk: "Would Leon push his way past terrible fear to save his friends?"

And Mimi: "And Leon Leafwing answered *yes, yes, yes* to all those questions…" She fluttered close to Leon and whispered, "And I never laughed at him. I loved him from the first moment I stared into his eyes."

Then Spider Kane spoke. "Leon, you went on a journey to find the Emperor Moth and to be with Mimi again. You have succeeded in both. But most important, along the way you found what you were truly looking for—*your own strength and courage*."

Leon turned to the five silhouettes standing before him in the early dawn light.

"Will you join us?" said Spider Kane.

"But what do you do?" said Leon.

"The Order of the MOTH is a secret band of bugs I formed after the Mosquito Wars," said Spider Kane. "Our purpose is to help those who are unable to help themselves. The initials M-O-T-H stand for Mission: Only to Help. We save water striders from flash floods and crickets from brush fires. We feed and educate orphaned ants. We find shelter for hiveless bees. We solve mysteries and fight injustice wherever we find it."

"Are there any other members?"

"Only the five of us," said Spider Kane.

"But what about Dr. Ant and Major General Bum?"

"Right here, lad," the Hawk said in Dr. Ant's falsetto. Then he saluted and hummed like General Bum, "Hmmmmm."

"You were *both* those guys?" said Leon.

"Mmm-hmm," said the Hawk.

"That explains why you were all wearing the same Italian shoes."

"Whoops," said the Hawk.

"You have a good eye, Leon," said Spider Kane, chuckling. "Now let me introduce you to Mimi's mother, Margaret."

"Thank you for finding my precious daughter, Leon," said Mimi in the nasal voice of the old butterfly.

"You?" Leon was truly stunned.

"Yes," said Mimi.

"And the so-called Ant Trilogy was merely three battered, second-rate novels Mimi really did find at a flea market," said Spider Kane. "And she found her rhinestone crown at the Bee City Thrift Store.

"The only robbery that actually occurred was the 'borrowing' of Midge Appleworm's scarf by Rosie. Since Midge has over two hundred silk scarves, we hoped she wouldn't be too much inconvenienced."

Leon gasped. He could hardly believe the complexity of the drama they had staged for his sake. "But what about all the other things that happened? The clicking noises?" he said.

"It's that time of year when deathwatch beetles click out their mating calls," said Spider Kane.

"But the mosquito patrols?"

"You can always count on mosquitoes being in the Forest in the summer," said Thomas Hawkins.

"What about the grub army?" asked Leon.

Spider Kane chuckled. "I merely coordinated our arrival at the stream with the annual Grub Day Parade."

Leon shook his head in astonishment.

"Good heavens, Leon," said Spider Kane. "Did you really think I knew the head size of a gossamer-winged butterfly?"

Leon began to laugh. He couldn't believe

Spider Kane and the others had gone to so much trouble just for him. As he laughed, Mimi slipped her hand into his. And the dawn wind felt softer and warmer.

"Will you join us, Leon?" said Spider Kane.

"Yes," breathed Leon. "Yes. Yes. Yes."

"Sure you want to fly with us, kid?" said the Hawk. "We've got some pretty dangerous adventures ahead."

"I'm flying," said Leon.

"Good, very good," said Spider Kane. Then he tightened one of the gloves on his hands. "Well, then, I must leave all of you now. I have some appointments to keep. But soon I'll return and gather you together."

"What do I do next?" piped Leon.

"Go back to the Cottage Garden with the others," said Spider Kane. "Relax. Celebrate. Then get ready."

"Ready?"

"Yes, Lieutenant Leafwing," said Spider Kane in his deep, velvety voice. "This has only been the beginning."

"Yes, sir," whispered Leon.

Spider Kane smiled. Then he threw a little salute to all of them and began crawling away. With his slight limp, he moved jerkily over the wet island grass.

"How will he get across the Dark Swamp?" asked Leon.

"Oh, there're plenty of bugs by the wharves—water boatmen and backswimmers," said Rosie. "One of them will carry him across. Spider Kane has friends everywhere."

In silence Leon and the others watched their mysterious commander disappear into the blinding light of the rising sun.

I'm like a poor fly;
Spiderman, please let me go.
I'm like a poor fly;
Spiderman, please let me go.
You got me locked up in your house,
And I can't break down your door.
                    —Bessie Smith
                       "The Spiderman Blues"

Spider Kane and the Mystery at Jumbo Nightcrawler's

CAST OF CHARACTERS
(in order of appearance)

LEON LEAFWING—An earnest young leafwing butterfly; a lieutenant in the Order of the MOTH

MIMI—A gossamer-winged butterfly; Leon's girlfriend; an actress and a lieutenant in the Order of the MOTH

THOMAS "THE HAWK" HAWKINS—The greatest living actor in the moth world; a lieutenant in the Order of the MOTH

LA MÈRE LEAFWING—Leon Leafwing's mother; formerly known as "Pupa"

WALTER DOGTICK—La Mère Leafwing's companion; a grubby but well-meaning old tick

SARATOGA D'BEE—Hostess and singer bee at Jumbo Nightcrawler's Supper Club on Waterfront Row

JUMBO NIGHTCRAWLER—Biggest worm on the waterfront; owner of a jazz supper club

JOHNNY ST. CLAIRE—Trumpet-playing housefly at Jumbo Nightcrawler's Supper Club

SPIDER KANE—Amateur sleuth; retired captain in the Mosquito Wars; jazz clarinetist; theater director; playwright; composer; leader of the Order of the MOTH; secret code name, "the Emperor Moth"

LITTLE PICKLES—Energetic, resourceful ladybug; a lieutenant in the Order of the MOTH; caterer and maker of tulip cradles

ROSIE—Little Pickles's partner; former lieutenant in the Mosquito Wars; member of the Order of the MOTH

RAYMOND JOHNSON—"The most wicked robber-fly on earth"; also known as the Bald Buzzer

HORNET GANG—Raymond Johnson's henchmen

Publisher's note: This is a work of fiction. Any resemblance to events, locales, or actual bugs (living or dead) is entirely coincidental.

PART I

❧ ONE ❧

Leon Leafwing sang softly to himself as he placed two honey drops on a rose-petal platter.

"No one to talk with,
All by myself."

He filled two buttercups with cherry juice and lit two beeswax candles.

"No one to walk with,
But I'm happy on the shelf.
Ain't misbehavin',
I'm savin' my love for you."

Leon moved two lima-bean-pod chairs close to each other. Then he fluttered to his mica mirror and fluffed up his tiny peach-colored ascot.

"I know for certain
The one I love."

He straightened the lapels on his summer

jacket and flicked a piece of dust from his brownish-orange butterfly wings.

"I'm through with flirtin',
It's just you I'm thinking of.
Ain't misbehavin'…"

Knock, knock, knock.

Leon threw open the door and sang, *"I'm savin' my love for you!"*

The blue gossamer-winged butterfly fluttered excitedly in the twilight. "Oh, Leon, isn't it thrilling?" she cried.

"Well," said Leon, puzzled. "It's actually a rather simple little dinner, darling, but…"

"Oh, you think he just wants to meet us for dinner?" Mimi rushed past Leon into his cabin. "I thought he wanted us for a mission—criminals on the waterfront, smugglers, pirates or something!"

"What?"

"I didn't even know that he was back. Did you? I can't wait to see him!"

"Who?"

"Spider Kane! You think we should leave

soon? I'm not quite sure where Jumbo Night-crawler's is, are you?"

"Wait, wait, wait!" said Leon. "What in the world are you talking about?"

Mimi caught her breath and stared at Leon. "Didn't you get a letter from him?" she said.

"Who? From who?"

"Spider Kane!"

"No, I didn't."

"Oh." Mimi looked confused.

"What letter? What are you talking about?"

"I found this letter in my mailbox just now." Mimi pulled a piece of blue paper from her purse and handed it to Leon. "I was sure you'd gotten one too."

By the flickering candlelight, Leon read the elegant handwriting on the note:

> Dear Mimi,
> At midnight meet me at Jumbo
> Nightcrawler's Supper Club on
> Waterfront Row. Please present this free
> pass to the hostess at the door.
>
> As ever,
> E. M.

The message was signed with the initials of Spider Kane's secret code name, Emperor Moth, and attached to it was a purple ticket with the word *free*. "I wonder why I didn't hear from him," said Leon.

"Did you look in your mailbox today?" Mimi asked.

"Yes, this morning."

"Well, let me check again."

As Mimi fluttered outside, Leon sat on one of his bean-pod chairs and stared at the note. For weeks now he had been living for a night such as this—a night when the mysterious Spider Kane would gather together his five lieutenants and lead them on a mission. Though Spider Kane was known throughout the Cottage Garden as an excellent detective, his Order of the MOTH was a well-kept secret. The abbreviation MOTH stood for Mission: Only to Help, because the spider had formed the band to help those who were unable to help themselves.

"Nothing in your mailbox," said Mimi, returning.

"Maybe he isn't including me on this mission

11

because I'm the newest and youngest member," Leon said.

"Don't be silly. We don't all have to get our orders at the same time. Spider Kane probably has another plan for you...some really special plan."

"Well, then, maybe I should just go with you anyway," said Leon. "Maybe—"

"I'm afraid not, honey," Mimi interrupted gently. "I've learned from experience that Spider Kane is very specific about his orders."

Leon didn't say anything. He just stared miserably at Mimi's note.

"Look at this wonderful dinner you've made for us!" Mimi said. "I don't have to leave this minute. We have time to eat together."

"I'm not very hungry," Leon mumbled.

"Oh, Leon, don't be sad," Mimi said. "Listen. Let's go visit Rosie and Little Pickles. Maybe they know what's going on."

Rosie and Little Pickles were both ladybug lieutenants in the Order of the MOTH.

"Okay."

"And will you save this lovely dinner for later?"

"I guess so."

Mimi kissed him. "Smile, kiddo," she whispered.

Leon gave her the teeniest smile.

"All right, let's go," she said, and she blew out Leon's two beeswax candles.

Night had fallen when Mimi and Leon left the twig cabin. They stood for a moment beneath the lemon-yellow moon and inhaled the sweet scent of honeysuckle.

"Ready?" Mimi whispered.

"Ready."

The butterflies raised their paper-thin wings and flickered into the balmy night sky. As they sailed above the Cottage Garden, they swooped over darkened patches of wild strawberries, over pasture roses, meadow clover, the Lily Pond, and an old sundial. Just beyond the stone birdbath they glided down to a tiny cottage under a moon-flower vine.

The cottage was the home of Leon's two best friends, Rosie and Little Pickles. When the two tireless ladybugs weren't flying special missions for Spider Kane, they were busy catering Garden parties or building tulip cradles for new Garden babies. Energetic and cheerful, they hated to waste even a second of their waking lives.

But when Leon and Mimi lit down near Rosie and Little Pickles's cottage, they found it completely dark. "Have they gone to bed early for once in their lives?" Mimi asked.

"I can't imagine," said Leon. It puzzled him that no smoke curled from the chimney. And no basket of cookies had been left on the front steps for night-working bugs. When he tapped on the door, it swung open. The cottage seemed very quiet and dark.

"Rosie! Little Pickles!" he called.

But there was no answer.

"Should we just go in?" said Mimi.

"I guess," said Leon, and he cautiously followed Mimi into the living room.

Mimi lit the lantern in the front window. As

she carried it about the cottage, shadows danced on tulip cradles, on dried herbs hanging from the low ceiling, and on leaf tins and flower plates stacked on the white-birch floor.

"Look!" said Leon, pointing to a nutshell bowl filled with mashed apple. On the floor was a tiny pile of apple peelings. "They must have left in the middle of baking."

"What's this?" said Mimi, and she grabbed a blue scrap of paper from the kitchen table. After she read it, she handed it to Leon.

Leon felt his heart sink as he read:

Dear Rosie and Little Pickles,
At mid night meet me at Jumbo
Nightcrawler's Supper Club on
Waterfront Row. Please present these
free passes to the hostess at the door.
As ever,
E. M.

Once again Spider Kane had signed the message with the initials of his secret code name, Emperor Moth. "I wonder why he doesn't want to meet with me," said Leon.

"I don't know, honey," said Mimi.

"You don't think he's changed his mind about making me a member of the Order of the MOTH, do you?" said Leon.

"Oh, no! Never! He's lucky to have you, and he knows it," said Mimi.

"I wonder if he sent a note to the Hawk too."

"I don't know. Do you want to go and find out?"

"Okay." Leon put the note back on the table. And with a sigh, he followed Mimi out of the ladybugs' cottage.

❧ TWO ❧

Hidden near the eastern wall of the Cottage Garden in a patch of meadow rue was the pebble estate of Thomas "the Hawk" Hawkins. Not only was the Hawk an outstanding lieutenant in the Order of the MOTH, he was also the greatest living actor in the moth world. Late at night he could often be found by his fire, reading plays and sometimes speaking the best parts aloud to himself.

But the Hawk's estate was nearly dark when Mimi and Leon arrived. Mimi rang the Hawk's doorbell and called his name, but there was no answer. She rang again.

Suddenly the door swung open. Mimi and Leon saw a horrible face leering at them from the shadows.

"Eek!" Mimi screamed.

"Don't be frightened, my dear," said a smooth, clear voice. "It's only a wooden mask exquisitely carved by the Harlequin Beetles of South America."

Mimi broke into her high little laugh. "Hawk!" she squealed. "You scared me to death!"

The great moth actor lowered the mask to reveal his own craggy, handsome face. "Hello, friends," he said.

Mimi gave the Hawk a big hug. "I'm so glad to see you! We heard your Asian theater tour was a huge success."

"Yes, yes, it was marvelous," said the Hawk. "The bugs turned out in droves to see our little plays."

"Rosie told me that you acquired some priceless treasures, too," said Mimi.

"Ah, she told you about my tapestry?"

"What tapestry?"

"The Moon Shadow Tapestry from the Tailor Ants of Borneo," the Hawk said in a hushed and reverent voice. "Only five of them were ever made. Come, I'll show you..." And he led Mimi and Leon into his house.

A beeswax candle burned in the foyer. The Hawk picked it up and carried it down the hall. As Mimi and Leon followed him, they fluttered past rare objects from all over the world. On other theater tours the Hawk had collected wax statues made by the Honeybees of China, beautiful fans made by the Sun Butterflies of New Guinea, and tin whistles made by the Australian Whistling Moths.

Finally, when they came to the Hawk's bedroom, he pointed to a needlepoint tapestry hanging near his feather bed.

"Oh! It's incredible!" breathed Mimi.

Leon wondered what the big fuss was about. The tapestry looked like an old rug with a picture of a couple of ants hugging in the moonlight.

"Don't let its simplicity fool you," said the Hawk, as if he had read Leon's mind. "The craftsmanship is unequaled anywhere in the world. You can't imagine my joy when I came upon it in a tiny shop in the hills of Borneo. And to think I got it for only a song."

"How fabulous!" said Mimi. "What song did you sing?"

"'Ducks on the Millpond,'" said the Hawk.

Mimi laughed her high little laugh again. "I'm not surprised they gave it to you," she said. "You have such a lovely voice."

Leon felt a pang of jealousy. Mimi had always admired *his* singing voice.

"So what are you two up to?" said the Hawk.

"Oh! I got a letter today from Spider Kane," said Mimi. "So did Rosie and Little Pickles. He wants us to meet him at midnight on Waterfront Row."

"Marvelous!" said the Hawk. "I got a message

19

from old E. M. myself. I was just getting ready to leave. Shall we all go together?"

"Well—I—" stammered Leon.

"Leon didn't get a note, Hawk," said Mimi quickly. "We can't figure out why. Do you know? Have you spoken to Mr. Kane?"

"No, but I'm sure Spy plans to include you in this new mission of his, Leon."

"How do you know?"

"He sent me a postcard recently. He's been in the North Country, you know, meeting with the United Ant Charities. But he wrote that as soon as he got back, he was going to call all of us together for an assignment—and he definitely included you."

"He did?"

"Of course. I'll prove it to you." The Hawk picked up a postcard from his dresser. Then he put on his reading glasses and read aloud:

"*My dear Hawk,*
I'm so glad to hear about your safe
return—and your wonderful treasure.
What a steal! Those ants are amazing,

aren't they? Please tell Rosie, Little
Pickles, Mimi, and Lieutenant Leafwing
that as soon as I'm back from my trip, I'll
be calling together our gang of six. After
we celebrate your success, I'll outline our
next little caper.

As ever,
E. M."

The Hawk took off his glasses and smiled at
Leon. "You see?" he said. "Spider Kane hasn't
forgotten *Lieutenant Leafwing*."

"Then why didn't he invite me to the supper
club tonight?" said Leon.

"I can't answer that, dear boy. But I do know
that Spy never does anything without a good
reason. Trust him."

"I guess you're right," said Leon, sighing.

The Hawk glanced at his pocket watch. Then
he put on his fedora. "Well, we'd better be going
or we'll be late...It's a bit of a journey to the
waterfront."

Mimi fluttered to Leon's side and gave him a
soft butterfly kiss. "If we don't fly off on a mission,

21

I'll come straight to your house after the meeting and tell you all about it, okay?"

"Okay," whispered Leon.

"Save that wonderful dinner you prepared for us."

"You bet," said Leon, trying to sound cheerful.

"*Au revoir*, my friend," said the Hawk gently. He tipped his fedora. Then he opened his wings and swept Mimi out the back door.

After Leon left the Hawk's estate, he flew as fast as he could over the Cottage Garden back to his twig cabin in the Wildflower Woods.

When he got home, he searched everywhere for his own blue note from Spider Kane. Maybe the wind had blown it out of his mailbox. Maybe it had fallen behind a hedge or was floating in his hickory rain barrel.

But there was no note. At last Leon went inside and lit his candles. Then he sat in his twig rocker and waited for Mimi.

As he rocked, Leon couldn't help picturing

his girlfriend sitting close to the handsome Hawk in a dark music club on Waterfront Row. And Rosie and Little Pickles, his two best friends, were with them! He pictured all of them receiving orders from Spider Kane while the band played and bugs danced and a singer sang about faraway places. It was almost more than he could bear.

Finally, before dawn, Leon washed the honey drops off his rose-petal platter. He poured the cherry juice back into an acorn jug. He took off his peach-colored ascot and his summer jacket. Then he blew out his candles.

As Leon lay on his pine-needle bed in the dark, he listened longingly to the night winds rustling the leaves outside. His heart was so heavy that when he finally fell asleep, he dreamed he was sinking like a stone to the bottom of the Garden Creek.

THREE

As soon as Leon woke up, he dashed next door to Mimi's burrow under the May-apple. When she didn't answer his knock, he peeked inside her front window. The little burrow looked as tidy as ever. A moss coverlet lay neatly on Mimi's straw bed. The bare earthen floor was swept smooth and clean. But there was no sign Mimi had returned from her meeting with Spider Kane.

Back home, Leon perched on his front step and watched for his gossamer-winged girlfriend. He also wistfully kept an eye out for Spider Kane. He pictured the elegant captain dressed in his gray cape, limping down the road toward the cabin. Two of the spider's legs had been wounded in the Mosquito Wars. But that had not prevented him from traveling all over the world investigating crimes or leading the Order of the MOTH, as well as playing jazz clarinet and directing theatrical productions.

Leon waited all morning, but Mimi never

came. Finally in the early afternoon he decided to find out if Rosie, Little Pickles, or the Hawk had returned from the meeting with Spider Kane. In the hazy, hot sunlight he flew across the Cottage Garden to the Hawk's pebble estate. When he found no one at home, he hurried to the ladybugs' cottage. But just as he'd expected, he found no one there, either.

When Leon returned home, he was too forlorn to putter in his garden or make a good dinner. He lay down on his pine bed and stared mournfully out the window.

It wasn't until the sun was going down that he spied a butterfly in the distance winging toward his cabin. Joy surged through him as he zipped out the door to greet Mimi. "Darling!" he shouted.

"Sonny!" answered the butterfly.

Leon moaned with disappointment. Not his darling Mimi, but his mother was fluttering toward him. La Mère Leafwing was wearing an orange kimono with an ostrich fern draped around her neck. She was carrying her tiny companion, Walter Dogtick. The barefoot tick wore his usual ill-fitting old coat.

"Wally and I are on our way to dinner, dearie," said La Mère, lighting down in Leon's yard. "We thought you might like to join us."

"No thanks, Mom," said Leon.

"Oh, sonny, I never see you anymore. Not since you insisted on getting your own place next to that tacky old butterfly," said La Mère. La Mère was quite jealous of Mimi and took every opportunity to insult her. She often brought up the fact that Mimi was a bit older than Leon.

"Moth-er..." warned Leon.

"Forgive me, forgive me!" La Mère said insincerely. "But you know, I'm lonely, dearie. I have no chums now except Wally." La Mère had been without friends ever since she'd had a falling-out with the Women's Bug Club.

"I know that, Mother. I feel bad about that. But—"

"Oh, don't worry about me!" interrupted La Mère. "But aren't you even slightly interested in why we're making a visit to Waterfront Row?"

"Waterfront Row?"

"Yes, we're going to Jumbo Nightcrawler's Supper Club."

"Jumbo Nightcrawler's Supper Club?"

"Yes, indeedy," said La Mère. "Wally and I are winging it to the wild side!"

"Dat's right, Pupa," said Walter Dogtick, calling La Mère by her childhood name. The two had grown up next to each other in the Goatweed Patch.

"But why—why are you going to Jumbo Nightcrawler's?" stammered Leon.

"Well, actually I received this rather odd invitation." La Mère handed a blue note to Leon and winked. "I think I have a secret admirer," she said.

Leon unfolded the paper and read:

> *Dear L. Leafwing,*
> *At midnight meet me at Jumbo*
> *Nightcrawler's Supper Club on*
> *Waterfront Row. Please present this free*
> *pass to the hostess at the door.*
>
> > *As ever,*
> > *E. M.*

"Oh! Oh! This is *my* note!" Leon shrieked.

"I beg your pardon?" said La Mère.

"This is mine! Mine! I'm sure of it! This was meant for me!" Leon was so excited he could barely contain himself.

"What are you talking about?" said La Mère huffily. "You know this E. M.?"

"He's—he's—" Leon sputtered. He couldn't reveal Spider Kane's secret code name to anyone, not even his own mother. "I'm—I'm not sure who he is," he said, "but I am sure this note was meant for me!"

"Well, I'm not so sure," said La Mère, pulling her ostrich fern about her.

"No, Mom, listen. This note is mine. Trust me. See, L. Leafwing could mean Leon Leafwing just as easily as La Mère Leafwing!"

"Yes, but it was sent to *my* address, dearie!" said La Mère, trying to snatch the note from Leon.

"I know, but that must have been a mistake. When did you find this in your mailbox?"

"This morning."

"Did you look in your mailbox yesterday?"

La Mère thought for a moment, then said, "No. I haven't been getting much mail lately." She sniffed pathetically.

"Oh, darn." Leon could have wept with disappointment. He was almost certain he was supposed to have received his note yesterday with all the others.

"Well, all you have to do is write me, dearie," said La Mère, misunderstanding Leon's disappointment.

"Yes, I know, Mother." Leon folded the note and put it in his pocket. Then he heaved a big sigh. "Well, can I go with you?" he said, hoping against hope that just maybe Spider Kane meant to meet with him alone that night.

"Of course!" said La Mère. "Let's *all* wing it to the wild side!"

❦ FOUR ❧

The Garden Creek ran along the southern border of the Cottage Garden. Hidden along its shore was the strange nightlife of Waterfront Row. From dusk until dawn night bugs and worms haunted the music clubs beneath the wild oats and foxtail grass.

Dogtick rode on La Mère's back, and Leon followed as they wove their way past dancing gnats rising and falling in the misty twilight. Oil lamps glowed in the leaf shanties that dotted the tiny hills and hollows around the creek.

Finally they let down in the cinnamon grass near Waterfront Row. "Where's Jumbo Nightcrawler's?" Leon asked.

"Follow me," said Dogtick, and he crept away into the mist.

La Mère and Leon fluttered after Dogtick until they came to the creek's edge. Tiny waves lapped against the soggy bank, and torches lit the entrance to a mud cavern.

"What a spooky place," said La Mère. "I hope the food's good."

"Precious, you'll be lucky if it's not *alive!*" said Dogtick.

"Oooooh!" squealed La Mère.

Inside, the club was jammed.

"May I help you?" said a husky voice. A glamorous-looking bee was standing by the door. She wore a long purple dress with a lilac cape, a blond wig, and rose-tinted glasses. Around her neck was a gold chain with a gold key.

"I believe I'm supposed to present you with this free pass," said La Mère, holding out her ticket.

The bee looked startled. Then she smiled. "Oh, yes, yes," she said. "Thank you."

"How 'bout making that pass good for all three of us, sweetheart?" said Dogtick, winking.

"Of course," said the bee. "Follow me."

As the bee led them across the sawdust dance floor, Dogtick said, "Who's playing tonight, sweetheart?"

"I'll be at the piano," said the bee. "And my friend, Johnny St. Claire, will be playing the trumpet."

"And your name, sweetheart?" said Dogtick.

"Saratoga," she said. "Saratoga D'Bee."

"Ah, lookin' forward to hearing ya, Ms. D'Bee," said Dogtick. "Nice hairdo you got there."

The bee smiled with embarrassment. "Thank you," she said. "Now, why don't you sit here? Your waiter will be right with you."

"Okey-dokey," said Dogtick.

After Saratoga D'Bee left them, La Mère looked around the club. "Let's all keep an eye out for this mysterious E. M.," she said.

But Leon was already desperately searching the smoky, dimly lit room for Spider Kane. Dragonflies and dance flies lined the juice bar on the side wall. Moths and caterpillars sat at tables or milled about the dance floor. Hornets and lightning bugs careened overhead.

But just as he expected, there was no sign of Spider Kane. Leon was sure that the members of the Order of the MOTH were all off on some great adventure. What rotten luck—not only had Leon's note been delivered to the wrong address, it had been discovered on the wrong day. He could hardly stand it.

Suddenly the crowd began to clap.

"Ooooh! Look at that big old thing!" said La Mère.

An enormous worm was moving across the stage, heading toward the microphone. He wore a panama hat, a white silk vest, and a flowered tie. A cigar was stuck in his mouth, and smoke curled up into the pink spotlight over his head.

"The Fat Worm himself," said Dogtick.

Jumbo Nightcrawler stood under the spotlight and surveyed the crowd through the haze of his cigar smoke. "Good evening, ladies and gentlemen," he said in a low, growly voice. "It is indeed a great pleasure to have you here in my club this fine summer evening. You bugs are looking mighty good out there tonight. Mighty good."

The bugs applauded for themselves.

"I'd like to remind y'all that tomorrow night we're hosting our annual talent show. Ms. D'Bee will be auditioning entries all afternoon. Then next weekend I'll be master of ceremonies at the

Lightning Bug Races. Of course, y'all know what I always say to start the race, don't you? *Ready, set, glow!*"

The audience moaned as the fat worm jiggled with laughter. "Okay, okay, I apologize. But now I'd like y'all to give a big round of applause for that powerful musical duo—our own Mr. Johnny St. Claire and your lovely hostess this evening, Ms. Saratoga D'Bee!"

A tuxedo-clad housefly carrying a shiny trumpet buzzed onto the stage. Following him was Saratoga D'Bee, the club's glamorous hostess. As the two performers bowed, the bugs clapped and whooped and pounded on the tables.

"The crowd is hot tonight," said Dogtick.

Saratoga sat at her piano. Then she leaned toward her mike and said in her husky voice, "I've got a new song I'd like to try out on y'all. Are you ready to go wild?"

"Yay!" the crowd screamed.

"Good," said Saratoga D'Bee. "Then let's all do the Bee House Stomp!"

Johnny St. Claire began tooting his horn, and Saratoga D'Bee began plunking her piano. As they played, bugs of all shapes and sizes swarmed onto the dance floor. The crowd moved their bodies in every possible way—they twisted, shimmied, slithered, buzzed, and stomped.

Leon stared unhappily at the crowd. Even the joyful music and rowdy atmosphere could not ease his terrible disappointment at being left behind by the Order of the MOTH.

Saratoga D'Bee began to sing:

"Policeman, policeman, don't catch me!
Catch that bug in the ostrich fern.
She took the money, I took none;
Put her in the bee house, just for fun."

Johnny St. Claire played a trumpet solo, puffing out his cheeks like tiny balloons. Saratoga answered with a long, steady piano roll. Then they played together—plunking and tooting. The piano rocked, and the platform swayed. An oil lamp on the mud wall cast great moving shadows of all the bugs doing the Bee House Stomp.

When the song ended, Saratoga D'Bee threw back her head and hollered, "Shoo fly!" And someone blew out the light.

In the dark the audience went wild, screaming and clapping.

When the noise finally died down, Dogtick cried, "That was great! Beautiful! Wasn't it, precious?"

But there was no answer. When the oil lamp flickered back on, Leon saw that his mother was not in her seat.

"Pupa?" Dogtick said. "Pupa?" He turned to Leon. "Where's your mother at?"

"I don't know," said Leon. "Maybe she stepped out for some air. I'll go check."

As Johnny St. Claire began playing a mournful solo, Leon wove his way through the slow-dancing crowd toward the door.

Just as he fluttered into the cool, damp night, a low-pitched voice came from behind him. "Wait."

Leon turned and saw a weird-looking character in a black hooded cloak. The creature's face was completely covered. As it moved jerkily toward him, Leon gasped and fled toward the water. But the creature came after him.

As Leon started to lift off into the weeds beside the creek, he caught his wing in a clump of bristle grass. He shook himself furiously, trying to get free. Suddenly the hooded monster leaped out of nowhere and landed on top of him.

Leon fought with all his might as the creature held on to him and whisked him into the bulrushes. "Help!" Leon screamed. "Help!"

"Be still!" his captor said in a deep, velvety voice. "Be still!"

"*Spider Kane!*" said Leon.

⋟ FIVE ⋞

"Shhh!" whispered Spider Kane.

"What—?" said Leon.

"Shhh! We have no time to lose. We have to find your mother. I need you to carry me into the air!"

"But —"

"Don't ask questions!" said Spider Kane as he quickly tied a cobweb thread to the butterfly. "Fly now! Fly!" he said.

In a daze Leon lifted off the ground into the misty dark. Spider Kane dangled below him as the two glided over the clubs on the mud bank — the Glowworm, Leo "Buzzy" Cicada's, the Hornflower Inn, and the King Cricket Casino.

Insect songs and peeper calls mingled with the music coming from the dance bands. Suave, neatly dressed mosquitoes hummed through the mist. Fireflies flashed mysterious signals to one another. And darkling beetles scuttled along the shore.

But Leon saw no sign of a matronly butterfly in an orange kimono. And he couldn't imagine why in the world Spider Kane had lunged out of the dark, searching for La Mère.

Suddenly Leon felt a tug. As he lit down on the lawn of the King Cricket Casino, he heard the *click, click, wheep, wheep* of the Cricket Brothers' Quartet.

"Quick, fly me over the creek and back," said Spider Kane. "They might have taken her by boat."

"Who?"

"I'll explain later. Hurry! Go!"

Leon lifted off the ground again and fluttered over the dark water, searching for small watercraft. *They might have taken her by boat*. What did that awful-sounding statement mean?

Leon felt another tug. Then he heard Spider Kane call, "Go back!"

When they had landed near Jumbo Nightcrawler's, Spider Kane started limping down the Bug Fishing Pier, which stretched into the creek. Finally he came to a halt and peered out over the water with a tiny reed telescope.

"What do you see?" Leon cried.

Spider Kane slowly lowered the telescope. "Absolutely nothing," he said, sighing.

"Where's my mother? What happened to her?" said Leon.

"I'm afraid she has been kidnapped," said Spider Kane.

"Kidnapped? By who?" gasped Leon.

"I'm not sure. It was quite dark, but I heard her cry out as several flying creatures whisked her out of the club."

"Flying creatures?" said Leon.

"Yes. Perhaps hornets...I wonder now if they might be related to the larger mystery that I am working on."

"Oh, you—you mean the mystery that made you send for everyone?" said Leon.

"I beg your pardon?"

"Is that why you sent us all those blue notes? Because of this larger mystery you're working on? Where is everyone? Where's Mimi and—"

"Wait," said Spider Kane. "What blue notes?"

"The blue notes that told us to meet you at Jumbo Nightcrawler's. Mine went to my mother, so I didn't—"

Suddenly Spider Kane grabbed Leon and held him firmly. "Stop, stop," he said. "Tell me *exactly* what you're talking about."

"I'm—I'm talking about the blue notes you sent to all the members of the Order of the

MOTH!" said Leon. "I got mine today. Did you mean for me to meet you today? Or yesterday with the others?"

"Leon! Where are the others now?" said Spider Kane.

"I don't know. They never came home. Don't—don't you know where they are?"

Spider Kane snarled with fury. Then he flung his black cloak around him and stalked off the Bug Fishing Pier.

Leon was overcome with terror. He'd never seen the spider in such a rage. He rushed after him. "What's wrong?" he cried. "What's wrong? Where is everyone?"

Spider Kane brought himself under control. Then he spoke in a low voice. "I don't know where they are," he said. "I only returned to the Garden this afternoon. All I know is that *I did not send any blue notes to anyone.*"

SIX

Leon stared at Spider Kane. Finally he breathed, "Then—then why are you here tonight?"

"While I was away, I was asked to investigate a waterfront crime," said Spider Kane. "I was going to call the Order of the MOTH together soon to help me. But first I wanted to do a little snooping on my own. However, it now seems someone has discovered my plan—and grabbed my lieutenants before I could gather them together."

"What?" said Leon, close to hysteria. "You mean Mimi—"

Suddenly a plaintive cry came from nearby. "Pupa? Pupa?"

"Good heavens," said Spider Kane, and he limped into the bulrushes as Walter Dogtick stumbled into view.

In the circle of light thrown by the supper club's torches, the tick looked lost. "Where's Pupa?" he asked, blinking at Leon.

"I don't know, Wally!"

"Where's she at?" said Dogtick.

"I *said* I don't know, Wally. I don't know!"

"You think she ran off with that E. M.?"

"No, Wally. Please, leave me alone!"

"I just wanted her to have a nice time," Dogtick said mournfully.

"I know, Wally. Now go away, please."

"Pupa? Pupa?" Dogtick called as he stumbled away into the night.

Fear and dread filled Leon as he stared after Dogtick. Where *was* his mother? Where was Mimi? Rosie? Little Pickles? The Hawk? What was going on? "Mr. Kane!" he said in a loud whisper.

Shadows of drift worms moved eerily along the foggy shore as the weeping strains of Johnny St. Claire's trumpet floated through the thick night air.

"Mr. Kane!" cried Leon.

"Here I am," said Spider Kane, limping out of the bulrushes. "Come, let's go back to my place. We must figure this out."

"Y-yes," said Leon, trembling.

Spider Kane attached a cobweb thread to the butterfly again. As they flew away from Waterfront Row, Walter Dogtick's lonely cry could be heard coming through the mist. "Pupa! Pupa!"

PART II

❧ SEVEN ❧

Leon and Spider Kane flew through the night to a crumbling stone wall on the south side of the Cottage Garden. After they had landed in the tall grass, the spider led the way through a tunnel in the wall to his elegant chambers.

Leon was still trembling with shock as Spider Kane lit the candelabra on his mantel and made a fire in his fireplace. When the dancing flames were casting shadows on the chalky walls, the spider turned to Leon. "Pull your chair close to the fire, son," he said. "It's a little chilly in here, isn't it?"

Leon did as he was told. Spider Kane changed into his paisley dressing gown and poured cherry juice into two touch-me-not goblets. After he had served Leon, he took out his briarwood pipe.

Spider Kane puffed silently for a moment, then said, "Now, let's go over this entire business one step at a time. First, the blue notes. What exactly did each note say?"

"I have the one my mother received." Leon reached in his pocket and pulled out the note that had been sent to La Mère. "The others say exactly the same thing," he said.

"Ah...let me see," said Spider Kane, taking the note from him. "Yes, that certainly is a good imitation of my handwriting. And somehow the forger knew my secret signature. Tell me—was *midnight* spelled as two words in all the notes that you saw?"

"Yes, I think so."

"And all the notes included a free pass to the club?"

"Yes."

"Hmm. What else can you tell me?"

Leon described his visit to Rosie and Little Pickles's cottage. "It was as if they'd dropped everything and rushed away," he said. "They even left mashed apple sitting in a nutshell bowl and apple peelings on the floor."

"Good heavens." The spider heaved a sigh. "Well, as I said before, I only returned to the Garden this afternoon. I've been in the North Country, meeting with the United Ant Charities. They have a case they'd like me to solve. As I said, I fully intended to enlist the assistance of the Order of the MOTH. But first I wanted to do a little investigating on my own."

"But why were you at Jumbo Nightcrawler's tonight?" said Leon.

"I was scouting for clues to the ant case. I planned to visit all the music clubs and keep my ears open for gossip about crimes that had taken place recently on the creek. The fact that I happened to be at Jumbo's to witness your mother's capture was pure coincidence."

Spider Kane looked again at the blue note that had been sent to La Mère. "So, whoever sent this note knew my secret signature..." His eyes closed for a moment. Then suddenly they shot open. "Aha!" he whispered fiercely. "Yes. Yes!"

"Yes what?" cried Leon.

"Wait!" Spider Kane jumped up, then limped across the room to his coat rack and grabbed a newspaper clipping from the pocket of his gray traveling cloak. "I want to read you an article from last week's *Garden Times*," he said. "It concerns the case I was starting to investigate on the waterfront." Then he read out loud:

More Bad News for the Ants

For ages, on the Atacama Desert of Chile, Harvester Ants have mined particles of fine gold. The hardworking, selfless ants have always kept only a tiny portion of the gold for themselves. The rest they send to the UAC (United Ant Charities). The UAC then sends the gold to a needy colony somewhere in the world. Recently, the Ant Kingdom in the Cottage Garden was chosen to receive the UAC's charity. As everyone knows, the Ant Kingdom suffered devastation from the spring-thaw mud slides this year. But as the UAC cargo ship was sailing down the Garden Creek, the gold was quietly stolen in the night. The sailor ant guarding the gold vanished also. It's believed that he was either taken hostage or thrown overboard. Sadly, the Ant Kingdom has lost out again.

When he had finished reading, Spider Kane sat down, relit his pipe, and stared at the fire.

Leon was confused. "I—I don't think we can worry about the ants until we find the other members of the Order of the MOTH," he said.

Spider Kane kept staring at his fire, deep in thought.

"Mr. Kane?"

When Spider Kane looked at Leon, his eyes were burning. "I could be wrong, Lieutenant, but I have a suspicion there's a connection between this mystery"—he rattled the newspaper clipping—"and the disappearances of our friends and loved ones."

"Wh-why?" asked Leon.

"Before I voice my suspicions, I need to study things a bit more." The spider stood. "Perhaps you should leave now, Leon, and get some rest. I have an important assignment for you tomorrow."

"You do? What?"

"I want you to go to the Hawk's house and Rosie's cottage and find their blue notes for me. But most important, when you're in the Hawk's house, search carefully for a postcard I sent him from the North Country last week."

"Oh, yes. He read that card to me."

"Excellent. I'm glad he saved it. Find it, please, and bring it to me."

"Yes, sir."

"Now go directly home," said Spider Kane as he accompanied Leon to the entrance of his chamber. "And be very careful, Lieutenant. We're not sure *who* or *what* we're dealing with."

There was no moonlight and no starlight. As Leon lifted into the sky, the coal-black dark trembled with mysterious sounds. *We're not sure who or what we're dealing with*. Terrified, Leon flew home as fast as he could.

The butterfly was still in a panic when he lit down at his twig cabin in the Wildflower Woods. As he unlocked his door, the wind picked up speed and seemed to whisper, *They're coming, they're coming.*

Leon rushed inside. After he locked his door, he pushed his jelly cupboard against it. Then without even lighting a candle, he dived into his soft, leafy bed.

As the wind moaned outside, Leon tried to imagine what had happened to Mimi, Rosie, Little Pickles, the Hawk, and his mother. He was afraid that any moment La Mère's kidnappers might burst into his house and snatch him, too.

Leon was so distraught that several times he got up and fluttered about the tiny one-room cabin. Finally he drove away his bad thoughts by pulling his covers over his head and imagining he was surrounded by a thick, protective butterfly cocoon.

✒ EIGHT ✒

Leon woke as soon as the first morning light filtered into his cabin. He immediately rushed next door to Mimi's. Peering through her window, he prayed that last night had been a bad dream. But there was no sign Mimi had returned to her little burrow.

With a heavy heart, Leon prepared to set off for the Hawk's estate to find Spider Kane's postcard. Just as he lifted into the hazy morning sky he heard cries of "Leon! Leon!"

Leon fluttered back to the ground and watched Walter Dogtick wobble toward him. The old tick looked more ill-kempt than ever. His coat was dragging along the ground, and his eyes were red and bleary. "Where's your mother at, Leon?" he cried. "Where?"

"I don't know, Wally."

"She didn't go back home to the Goatweed Patch. She didn't visit the Flowerpot District. No one's seen her, Leon. Did she run away with that E. M.?"

"No, absolutely not, Wally. E. M. is a friend of mine. I've talked to him. He hasn't seen her."

"Well, why did he tell her to meet him at Jumbo Nightcrawler's?"

"He didn't, Wally. That was a trick."

"A trick? Whadya mean? Who tricked her?"

Leon was afraid to tell Dogtick about the flying creatures taking La Mère away. It was all too confusing at this point. "I don't know, Wally."

"Maybe she was playing a trick on me," said Dogtick. "Maybe she wanted to escape from me because I'm so grubby."

"No, Wally, no."

"Why not?" said the tick. "I'd run away from me too, if I could." And with a self-loathing moan, Dogtick crept off into the Wildflower Woods.

"Wally, don't blame yourself!" called Leon. "Wally!"

But Walter Dogtick kept going without looking back.

When he arrived at the Hawk's estate, Leon slipped through the door and fluttered down the hall. He passed the wax statues from China and the fans from New Guinea.

Then in the Hawk's bedroom, he stared for a moment at the rare Moon Shadow Tapestry from Borneo. The little ants embracing in the moonlight reminded him of himself and Mimi. "Oh, darling, where are you?" he whispered tearfully.

Leon finally turned away from the tapestry and began searching for the Hawk's blue note and the postcard Spider Kane had sent the moth from the North Country. Leon found them both on the dresser. Just as he put them in his pocket, he heard an ominous sound—*Hmmmmmmmm.*

Leon fluttered to a corner. Then he protected himself as his leafwing ancestors had done for eons: he folded his wings above his back, making himself look like a dead leaf.

Hmmmmmmmm.

Leon opened one eye and nearly fainted with horror. Four hornets were gliding down the Hawk's hallway. A fat hornet paused to look behind the South American masks. A skinny hornet looked under the New Guinea fans. A tall hornet shook the Chinese statues. A short hornet studied the Moon Shadow Tapestry.

"It ain't here, fellas," said the tall one.

"The boss says we gotta find it," said the skinny one.

"He'll flip out if we don't," said the short one.

"Benny's right, it ain't here," said the fat one. "Let's beat it."

Then the four hornets zipped out the back door.

When the coast was clear, Leon fled from the lonely mansion as fast as he could. As he sailed over the Cottage Garden, he wondered why the hornets had been snooping about the Hawk's estate. Who was the "boss" they had spoken of? And what had he ordered them to find? Leon was desperate to tell Spider Kane about the four prowlers, but first he had to retrieve Rosie and Little Pickles's blue note.

When Leon entered the ladybugs' cottage under the moonflower vine, he found it more forlorn than ever. The little clay oven was not sending out its usual odors of cinnamon and nutmeg. The air was not filled with the sounds of ladybug laughter. Dust had gathered everywhere. The mashed apple in the nutshell bowl had turned dark brown.

Leon found the blue note on the kitchen

table. Just as he grabbed it, he heard that noise again. *Hmmmmmmmm.*

Leon quickly hid behind the kitchen table. Once again, he folded his wings above his back to make himself look like a dead leaf. Then as he held his breath, he saw the same four hornets glide through the front door.

The hornets began prowling about the sitting room. The skinny one looked under the cornhusk sofa. The fat one peered inside the pie safe. The tall one looked inside the tiny clay oven. The short one examined the tulip cradles.

Suddenly there was a noise outside.

"Hey, someone's coming!" said the thin one.

"Let's get outta here!" said the fat one.

"Go! Get! Beat it!" said the tall one.

"Move!" said the short one.

The four hornets scooted out the front door just as the back door opened. Leon stayed frozen to the spot, wondering what awful creature was going to break into the cottage next.

Flick-flack, flick-flack came the sound of wing strokes. The noise was wonderfully familiar!

"Little Pickles!" Leon cried as a tiny, plump ladybug wearing a red shawl flickered into the kitchen.

"Leon! You scared me to death! What are you doing here?" said Little Pickles.

"What are you doing here?" Leon said.

"Oh, I had to take care of Aunt Lila. Her house caught fire Saturday. And she lost nearly everything. I helped her get situated with her sister, Bootie. See, Bootie lives in—"

"Excuse me, Little Pickles," Leon interrupted. "But where's Rosie? Did she go with you?"

"No. Isn't Rosie back yet?" said the ladybug, glancing about.

"Where is she, Little Pickles? When did you see her last?"

"Oh. The day before yesterday. She left to cater a party. Then she was going to meet Mr. Kane at Jumbo Nightcrawler's Supper Club. I was supposed to join her there at midnight. But in the middle of baking, I got word about Aunt Lila. Oh, horrors," said Little Pickles as she stared at the nutshell bowl filled with apple.

"What a mess..." She began to tidy up.

"Wait, wait a minute," said Leon. His voice was shaking. "Listen to me, Little Pickles."

The ladybug took one look at the butterfly and dropped her apron.

"Come in here," Leon said, and he led Little Pickles into the front room. He quickly peeked out the window to make sure the hornets were not outside. Then he pulled the curtains shut and lit down next to the ladybug on the sofa.

"I have some bad news..." he began. He told her all about the kidnapping of La Mère. He told her about running into Spider Kane. He told her about all the blue notes being fakes. He told her about the hornet intruders. And last of all, he told her that Rosie and the others had not been seen for two days.

When he finished, Little Pickles looked stunned. "You—you mean Rosie's disappeared?"

Leon nodded sorrowfully.

"And you think she and the others might have been captured like your mother? By those awful hornets?"

"Maybe," said Leon.

"Oh." Little Pickles stared at him with wide, desperate eyes. "I—I feel like screaming," she said.

"Go ahead and scream, Miss Pickles," said a deep, velvety voice. Then Spider Kane limped through the open back door into the sitting room.

"Oh, Mr. Kane!" said Little Pickles. But instead of screaming, she burst into tears.

❧ NINE ❧

"There, there," said Spider Kane as he patted the distraught ladybug on the back. "I thought I would find you here, Miss Pickles. When I reviewed the evidence of your departure, I realized you would never leave mashed apple in a bowl or apple peelings on the floor. Unless, of course, you were rushing off to help someone in immediate danger. If you'd left to join me on a mission, you'd surely have cleaned your cottage first."

"That's true," said Little Pickles, sniffing. "I wanted to bake a pie for everyone and clean the cottage before I joined you on the mission. But then I got word about Aunt Lila's fire. See, she lost—"

"Excuse me for interrupting, Little Pickles," said Leon. "But I have to tell Mr. Kane something important!"

"Indeed? What?" said the spider.

"Four hornets broke into the Hawk's place! Then they came over here!" Leon went on to explain about the four prowlers in the Hawk's estate and Little Pickles's cottage.

"And that's all you can remember of their conversation?" said Spider Kane.

"Yes," said Leon. "I just remember one of them saying, 'The boss says we gotta find it.' And another saying, 'He'll flip out if we don't.'"

Spider Kane stood and began pacing about the living room, lost in thought.

"Who's their boss?" asked Little Pickles.

Spider Kane shook his head absently, then paused to glance out the window. "Good heavens," he exclaimed. "Someone else is heading this way now. I believe it's—yes, it is—it's the singer from Jumbo Nightcrawler's."

"Saratoga D'Bee?" said Leon.

"Yes. Quick, Leon, hide with me," said Spider Kane. "Miss Pickles, the bee must be coming to see you. Do not reveal *any*—I repeat, any— information to her. Say as little as possible. Let her do all the talking."

"Yes, sir." The tiny ladybug quickly pulled herself out of her grief and assumed a military air.

"Into the kitchen, Leon—" said Spider Kane. And he hurriedly led the butterfly into the kitchen, where they hid behind the cream-colored curtains.

A moment later, Leon heard a knock at the front door. Then he heard Little Pickles say, "Yes?"

"Are you Miss Little Pickles?" came a husky-sounding voice.

"Yes."

"My name is Saratoga D'Bee. I must talk to

you. I have a terrible confession to make. May I come in?"

"Yes."

Leon heard the door close. Then he heard the buzzing and flick-flacking of wings. He peeked out from behind the kitchen curtain just long enough to see the bee and the ladybug light down on the sofa.

Wearing a black silk cape, her rose-tinted glasses, and her blond wig, Saratoga D'Bee was fiddling nervously with the gold key that dangled from the chain around her neck. When she looked up at Little Pickles, Leon quickly hid behind the curtain again.

"I had to do it," the bee suddenly blurted out. "I didn't want to, but I had to! He made me."

"Yes?" said Little Pickles.

"Yes. See, I helped your friends get captured, Miss Pickles. I found out who they were when I collected their free passes at the door—he planned it so they'd be the only ones with free passes, of course. And then I had to identify all of them to the hornets with my songs."

"Yes?" said Little Pickles.

"Oh, yes, I'm so disgusted with myself," said the bee. "Take the leafwing, for instance. She was wearing this tacky ostrich fern, so I put it in my song:

> *'Policeman, policeman, don't catch me!*
> *Catch that bug in the ostrich fern.*
> *She took the money, I took none;*
> *Put her in the bee house, just for fun.'*

The 'ostrich fern' tipped off his gang of hornets. So when the lights went out, they grabbed her and took her off."

"Yes?" said Little Pickles.

"Yes! And the same thing happened to the others the night before. I sang about the moth's fedora. I sang about the butterfly's blue wings. I sang about the ladybug's hand-knitted shawl. Then they each got taken away too."

"Ye-es." Little Pickles's voice wobbled a bit. But she cleared her throat.

"Oh, please believe me when I say I didn't want to help him! He forced me, see? But they're all okay, I promise you!" said the bee.

"Only I can't tell you where they are because I don't have any idea where they are."

"Yes?" said Little Pickles.

"Yes!" said the bee. "And please don't ask me who *he* is. I can't tell you that, either. He'd seek terrible revenge if he ever found out that I squealed on him."

"Yes?"

"Oh, yes, he's very wicked, Miss Pickles. You're probably wondering how I got hooked up with a creep like that in the first place. See, I used to be his girlfriend. I was just a mixed-up young thing. But when I got smart, I escaped to the waterfront and got a job at Jumbo Nightcrawler's. Jumbo's a doll. Johnny St. Claire is too. So when I started singing there, I felt like I'd found my true home at last."

"Yes," said Little Pickles.

"Everything was going great until the creep found me. He wanted me to help him kidnap your friends. He threatened to tell Jumbo about my past and get me fired. But worse, he threat-ened—"

"Yes?" said Little Pickles.

"To harm my three little bees. I—I have three adorable little bees, Miss Pickles. They're staying with my mother now. Let me show you their picture..."

"Yes," said Little Pickles.

"See...that's Bubba, Natalie, and—and my baby, Mike." Leon heard the bee sniff, then blow her nose. He thought he heard Little Pickles sniffling too.

"You got a good heart, Miss Pickles," said the bee in her husky voice.

"Yes."

"So you see why I'm so afraid of him? You see why I went along with him and sang all those dreadful songs that identified his victims to the hornets?"

"Yes," said Little Pickles.

"Thank you for understanding," said the bee. "But now I feel so guilty and dreadful. We got to work together to get your friends free and to get this creep outta our lives for good!"

"Yes!" said Little Pickles.

"There's only one thing that will send him packing," said the bee. "He keeps talking about gold. He keeps talking about someone named E. M. It seems your friends—and this E. M. character—know about some shipment of gold that he meant to steal for himself. I don't know what he's talking about. But if you know, could you bring this gold to me so I could give it to him? We've got to do something to help your friends. And to help keep my Bubba, Natalie, and Baby Mike from his clutches—" The bee burst into hysterical crying.

"Yes, yes, yes," said Little Pickles soothingly.

"You'll help?" said the bee.

"Yes."

"Oh, thank you, Miss Pickles! I'm just glad they didn't get you too. Were you out of town or something?"

"Yes."

"Well, lucky for you—and E. M., whoever that is," said the bee. "If you know this E. M., Miss Pickles, I hope you'll be telling him everything I told you. I don't know how long the creep's patience is going to hold out..."

"Yes."

"I hope E. M. understands the situation. I mean, if it was up to you and me, we'd quick give up the gold to save the lives of our loved ones. Am I right?"

"Yes."

"All the gold in the world is worthless if our loved ones aren't safe and sound. Am I right?"

"Yes."

The bee paused for a moment as if waiting for Little Pickles to say more. Then she said, "Well! I must get back. I promised Jumbo I'd audition the talent for tonight's talent show."

"Yes," said Little Pickles.

"It's been great talking to you, Miss Pickles. You're a very good listener."

"Yes."

Buzzzzz. Flick-flack.

"Good-bye, Miss Pickles. I hope we can meet again sometime—under better circumstances, of course."

"Yes."

Then the door softly closed.

"Whew!" said Little Pickles.

"Aha!" cried Spider Kane, leaping out from behind the kitchen curtains. "Aha! Aha!" The spider laughed happily to himself as he limped around the room, clenching his fists and shaking his head.

"What is it, Mr. Kane?" cried Leon.

"That poor bee!" cried Little Pickles. "What in the world was she talking about?"

"What creep? What gold?" said Leon. "Did she mean the ants' gold?"

"Yes, I believe so, I believe so," said Spider Kane. Then he looked sharply at Leon. "Lieutenant, did you collect the blue notes and the postcard?"

"Yes, here they are," said Leon, handing them over.

"Ah, good! Thank you." The spider glanced at the postcard. "Yes!" he said with a broad smile. "Well, I must leave you now."

"Oh, no, please!" said Leon. "Don't go now! Tell us what's going on. We have to save Mimi

and my mother now or else that creep might—"
He was too upset to go on.

"Yes, please help us, Mr. Kane!" said Little
Pickles. And she started to weep again.

"Forgive me," Spider Kane said gently to
both of them. "But I'm afraid I need just a bit of
time to sort things out. Then later, I'll explain
everything."

"But this can't wait until later!" said Leon.

"What if this creep decides to do away
with all of them before nightfall?" cried Little
Pickles.

But Spider Kane pulled his gray cloak
around him. "Rest assured that our friends and
loved ones will not be done away with so soon.
Not as long as this 'creep' believes they are his
only link to the gold."

"What do they have to do with the ants'
gold?" said Leon.

Spider Kane held up one hand. "If you will
both come to my chambers tonight at seven, I
will give you a hot dinner. And *then* I'll serve up
some cold facts." Before Leon and Little Pickles

could protest, the spider saluted them and limped out of the cottage.

❧ TEN ❧

Promptly at seven o'clock Leon and Little Pickles arrived at Spider Kane's crumbling stone quarters.

"Come in," said the spider as he greeted them in his paisley dressing gown. "Let's go into the dining room and enjoy our meal."

"I'm afraid I don't have much of an appetite," said Little Pickles.

"Me neither," said Leon. "Can't you tell us what's going on first?"

"No, no, you must both take some nourishment before we attend to business matters. Come with me," said Spider Kane softly. And he led his two distraught lieutenants into his elegant dining room.

"Oh, my," said Little Pickles as she stared at the candlelit dinner waiting for them: pumpkin soup, a wild rose and nutmeat casserole with cranberry dressing, potato salad with chestnuts, poppy-seed cakes, and hot cinnamon rolls.

"Sit," said Spider Kane simply, and they did.

Throughout the meal none of them spoke, except to request a dish or offer thanks to the one who passed it. Leon was surprised to discover how hungry he actually was, for he had not eaten in two days.

Finally, when the last of the acorn-cap bowls had been cleared away and only the touch-me-not goblets filled with iced cocoa remained, Spider Kane pressed cherry-leaf tobacco into his pipe and said, "All right now, let's begin. First, I would like to share with you what I believe to be *the very key to the entire mystery.*" He reached into the pocket of his dressing gown and pulled out a postcard.

"That's the postcard you sent to the Hawk, isn't it?" said Leon. "What has that got to do with —"

Spider Kane held up a hand. "Wait, please.

Read it out loud, Lieutenant." He handed the card to Leon, then puffed on his pipe as Leon read:

"My dear Hawk,
I'm so glad to hear about your safe
return—and your wonderful treasure.
What a steal! Those ants are amazing,
aren't they? Please tell Rosie, Little
Pickles, Mimi, and Lieutenant Leafwing
that as soon as I'm back from my trip, I'll
be calling together our gang of six. After
we celebrate your success, I'll outline our
next little caper.

As ever,
E. M."

"Now," said Spider Kane. "Assume for a moment that *the creep* Ms. D'Bee spoke of has a very good reason to be interested in the goings-on in the Cottage Garden. Suppose the creep decides one of the best ways to get private information is to read the mail of other bugs, and he sneaks aboard the Garden mailboat. When he riffles through the mail, he comes across this postcard. What could he learn from it?"

"Well, perhaps that you were on a trip, and that you'd be back soon," said Little Pickles. "I should think that's about all."

"Think again, Miss Pickles," said Spider Kane. "First, the card allows our creep to study my handwriting. Second, it reveals my secret initials. Third, and most important, it provides him with the names of the members of the Order of the MOTH. Though in your case, Leon, the creep made a mistake. On the card I purposely refer to you as 'Lieutenant Leafwing' to celebrate your newly acquired title. The creep, however, must have assumed your mother was the lieutenant in your family. After all, you're quite young to be a lieutenant in any regular army."

"I told my mother that note was meant for me!" said Leon.

"And you were right," said Spider Kane. "Now, you may both wonder why this so-called creep would want to copy my handwriting. And why would he care about my secret initials? What does it matter who I name in the card?

The reason is that our creep misunderstands three little lines in this card. And his misunderstanding has been disastrous for us."

"What did he misunderstand?" said Leon.

"Wait," said Spider Kane. He picked up a newspaper clipping. "I'll get back to our creep and his misunderstanding in a moment. But first, Leon, permit me to explain to Miss Pickles the information I shared with you last night."

"What?" said Little Pickles.

"This is an article from last week's *Garden Times*. It is titled 'More Bad News for the Ants,' and it begins by telling us about the Harvester Ants of the Atacama Desert of Chile—"

"Oh, yes. I know about those wonderful ants," said Little Pickles. "They mine gold, then give most of it to the United Ant Charities to help needy ants. Rosie and I have done volunteer work for the UAC."

"I'm not surprised," said Spider Kane. "Perhaps you've heard then that the UAC's cargo ship was robbed on its way to the Ant Kingdom?"

"Oh, dear!" said Little Pickles.

"Yes," said Spider Kane. "And it seems that the sailor ant guarding the gold vanished also. It's believed he was drowned or taken hostage."

Little Pickles shook her head. "What is this world coming to?" she said sadly.

"I'm afraid I don't know," said Spider Kane. "Well, now, let's go back to our creep and his misunderstanding. Please allow me to turn back to my postcard and reread three lines." He picked up the card and read again:

> *"My dear Hawk,*
> *I'm so glad to hear about your safe return—*
> *and your wonderful treasure. What a*
> *steal! Those ants are amazing, aren't*
> *they?..."*

"Of course, those lines refer to the Moon Shadow Tapestry the Hawk acquired from the Tailor Ants of Borneo," said Spider Kane. "But what do you suppose our creep thought?"

"Oooh," breathed Leon. "He thought you were referring to the ants' stolen gold!"

"Precisely," said Spider Kane. "Therefore, I

believe our creep has no knowledge whatsoever of the Order of the MOTH. Instead, he was after a gang of gold thieves."

"Oh! Now I understand what Ms. D'Bee meant when she kept talking about that gold!" said Little Pickles.

"Amazing!" said Leon. "But who is this creep, Mr. Kane?"

"If my suspicions are correct, he is a creature who will stop at nothing to get what he wants," said Spider Kane softly. "He is a creature who will use all his talents and skills to manipulate others. He is a creature who is known in the underworld as the Bald Buzzer. But his real name is Raymond Johnson."

"Raymond Johnson?" said Leon.

"Yes. Raymond Johnson is a robber-fly," said Spider Kane. "And quite possibly the most wicked robber-fly on earth."

ELEVEN

Leon and Little Pickles stared at Spider Kane. "How—how do you know about this robber-fly?" gasped Leon.

"I first heard about Raymond Johnson some time ago when I began performing in New Orleans," said Spider Kane. "Raymond Johnson was a legend on the Mississippi, for he had once been a fantastic entertainer. When he sang, he sang with total abandon. The music took over his whole body. Often, he couldn't keep from hurling himself about the stage—sometimes even into the audience. In fact, one night he tragically hurled himself right into a beach-party bonfire. He survived, but all the bristly hairs on his body were singed off."

"How awful," said Little Pickles.

"In spite of his accident, Raymond Johnson continued to perform. Bugs from miles around came to see him. He had a great talent for turning old-fashioned nursery songs into electrifying numbers."

"How original," said Little Pickles.

"Yes. The robber-fly had a great future ahead of him—until he got involved with the Hornet Underworld."

"The Hornet Underworld?" gasped Little Pickles.

"Yes. The hornets became great fans of his and gradually began to lure him into their criminal activities. It wasn't long before the talented robber-fly quit singing altogether and began hanging out full-time with the hornet thugs. His new cronies nicknamed him 'the Bald Buzzer'— due to his hairless condition, no doubt. And they convinced him to join them in acts of piracy along the river. Soon the Bald Buzzer became the toughest, meanest member of the gang."

"What did he do?" asked Leon.

"He attacked families sailing downriver— defenseless little bugs looking for a better way of life in the south. From all I heard, Raymond Johnson, or the Bald Buzzer, took a certain glee in stealing from these harmless creatures. Often he sank their tiny boats, leaving them stranded and penniless."

"Oh, how awful!" said Little Pickles angrily.

"Yes, it is awful," said Spider Kane. "And the waste of a tremendous talent."

"Well, what makes you think that the Bald Buzzer was after the ants' gold shipment?" said Leon.

"That conclusion was actually reached by the United Ant Charities," said Spider Kane. "Their investigators reported that Raymond Johnson and his gang of hornets were recently sighted in Santiago, Chile."

"Santiago, Chile?" said Leon.

"Yes, the ant port nearest the desert where the Harvester Ants' gold originated. Next, Johnson was spotted in the North Country where the gold was first delivered. And then more recently, he was seen near the Garden Creek. Therefore, the United Ant Charities suspects that Raymond Johnson was pursuing the gold all the way from Chile to the Cottage Garden."

"Oh, I see!" said Little Pickles. "But you

don't think he was the one who stole the gold?"

"No, I believe now that when he finally caught up with the ant cargo ship, he discovered that someone else had beaten him to it. He scoured the waterfront for clues, until my post-card threw his suspicions on our 'gang of six.' At that point he decided to capture all of you. So he sent out his blue notes and enlisted the help of Ms. D'Bee."

"Gracious!" said Little Pickles. "Everything makes sense now. Since the others can't seem to tell him where the gold is, he wants me to lead him to 'E. M.' and the gold!"

"Precisely," said Spider Kane.

"But who do you think really stole the gold?" asked Leon.

"That is the mystery we must solve later—when the Order of the MOTH is reunited," said Spider Kane. "In the meantime, our first concern must be rescuing our friends...before it is too late."

"Too late?" squeaked Leon.

"Yes," said Spider Kane. "You see, Raymond

Johnson will go to any lengths to get what he wants. He is brilliant, selfish, and totally ruthless."

"That—that means he might really hurt Mimi, Mom, and the others?" said Leon.

"Of course he will," whimpered Little Pickles. "And they don't even understand what he wants from them!"

"What can we do, Mr. Kane?" said Leon.

"All right. Let's suppose that Ms. D'Bee's creep is, in fact, Raymond Johnson, and that she is correct when she says that only he knows where the captives are. It seems obvious, then, that we must find Johnson before we can find our friends. And we must find him immediately. Tonight, in fact."

"Tonight?" said Leon.

"Yes," said Spider Kane, rising.

"But where will we find him?"

Spider Kane limped to his writing desk and took out his feather fountain pen. He quickly scribbled a note and handed it to Little Pickles.

The ladybug read the note out loud:

"Dear Mr. Johnson,
Meet me at Jumbo Nightcrawler's
tonight. I think I have something you
want.

Signed,
E. M."

"You must take this message to Ms. D'Bee at once," Spider Kane said to Little Pickles. "Tell her to deliver it to the creep she spoke of. Then meet Leon and me on the Bug Pier."

"What do we do then?" said Leon.

"We go into the club and wait for Mr. Raymond Johnson to show up. And then we will throw our net over him. Raymond Johnson has woven a web around the Order of the MOTH, and now it is our turn to weave *our* web around *him*."

"But if he thinks we're bringing him the gold, won't he just kidnap us too?" said Little Pickles.

"Not if he can't identify us," said Spider Kane.

"But Saratoga can identify me," said Little Pickles. "I'm afraid she might be so frightened of him, she'll spill the beans."

"That is why you're going to wear a disguise," said Spider Kane. "And to be on the safe side, Leon and I will disguise ourselves also."

"How?" said Leon.

Without a word, Spider Kane limped to the old army footlocker at the end of his bed. He lifted the lid and began pulling out bits and pieces of costumes—wigs, berets, V-shaped beards, and several pairs of dark glasses. "Miss Pickles, can you play the drums?" he asked.

"No, but I've always wanted to."

"Good. Tonight you'll get your chance," said Spider Kane. "And when I introduce you in the talent show, your name will be Lady Jam."

"Gracious! You mean *we're* going to perform in the talent show at Jumbo Nightcrawler's?" said Little Pickles.

"Precisely. Leon, you play the piano, don't you?" said Spider Kane.

"A bit."

"Good. Your name will be Kid Ivory."

"Kid Ivory?" said the butterfly. "And—and who will you be?"

"Me?" Spider Kane put on a beret and dark glasses. He picked up his clarinet and tooted a jazzy string of notes. Then he lowered his horn and raised his eyebrows at Leon and Little Pickles. "In Paris and New Orleans," he whispered, "I'm known as Doctor Legs."

PART III

❧ TWELVE ❧

Thunderflies swarmed above the Garden Creek. As Leon and Spider Kane waited on the Bug Fishing Pier for Little Pickles, they heard the teeny flies whispering furiously, "Storm a-comin', storm a-comin'!"

Just as Leon was beginning to think that the ladybug would never show up, he heard the *flick-flack* of her wings. Then Little Pickles bumped down onto the pier, gasping for breath. "Mission accomplished!" she said.

"Yes, Miss Pickles?" said Spider Kane.

"What did Saratoga say?" asked Leon.

"Oh! She was so excited she started to shake," said Little Pickles. "She said that if E. M. turned over the gold, she was sure the creep would set everyone free, and that he would stop threatening her children. Then she rushed off to give him the note."

"Good work, Miss Pickles," said Spider Kane.

"Now, where's my disguise?" said the ladybug. "You two look wonderful!"

Leon had to agree with her. When he'd looked in the mirror earlier, he'd hardly recognized the cool-looking butterfly in the dark shades staring back at him. He and Spider Kane were both wearing sunglasses, tuxedos, and tiny false goatees.

"How do I look?" said Little Pickles, pulling on a long wig.

"Let's hide your face a bit more, Lady Jam," said Spider Kane. He pulled a few strands of the red wig over her face. "There," he said. "Now, get ready, Bugland. Here comes the Doctor Legs Trio."

Thunder cracked the sky and a light rain was falling as Spider Kane, Leon, and Little Pickles entered Jumbo Nightcrawler's Supper Club. In the front hall they found Saratoga D'Bee and

Johnny St. Claire. Saratoga held a clipboard and pen. Beside her was a piece of slate that read:

TALENT SHOW TONIGHT —
eight o'clock till mid night

"Good evening, how are y'all tonight?" Saratoga said, smiling.

Leon thought the bee looked lovely in her apple-green evening dress with the matching cape. Her gold-key necklace dangled around her neck. She wore her rose-tinted glasses, and a tiny lilac bud was pinned to her blond wig.

"Very well, thank you," said Spider Kane. "Lady Jam, Kid Ivory, and I would like to enter your talent competition."

"Oh, yes?" Saratoga glanced at Spider Kane and Leon. But her gaze seemed to linger on Little Pickles. "Have I seen you perform somewhere before?" she asked the ladybug.

"I don't think so," said Little Pickles in a high voice. Then she coughed and turned her head away.

"I doubt you have seen any of us, madame," said Spider Kane quickly. "We have performed publicly only in New Orleans."

"Wait a minute...wait one minute!" said Johnny St. Claire. "I know this guy! I recognize that voice!"

Leon froze with fear.

"Who is he, Johnny?" said Saratoga D'Bee, staring intently at Spider Kane.

"He's Doctor Legs!" said Johnny. "The best clarinet player I've ever heard! I almost didn't recognize you with that beard, Doc!"

Spider Kane smiled. "You've seen me perform, Johnny?" he said.

"I'll say! My dad is Earl St. Claire. He used to play bass with you in New Orleans!"

"Good heavens," said Spider Kane, grinning. "I remember Earl. A fine musician."

"Thank you for saying that," said Johnny. "Tell me, are you performing here tonight?"

"If the good bee here will allow it," said Spider Kane, nodding at Saratoga D'Bee.

"Oh, you've gotta put these folks on the list, Saratoga!" said Johnny St. Claire. "Doctor Legs is dynamite."

"It sounds as if you're more than an amateur, Doctor Legs," said Saratoga D'Bee. "I'm afraid our local entertainment might not stand a chance in the competition."

"Don't include us in the competition," said Spider Kane. "We'd just like to try out some new material we've been working on."

"Well, all right," Saratoga said, smiling. "I enjoy good music as much as the next bug. Show them to a table, Johnny."

As Spider Kane started into the club, he leaned toward Saratoga D'Bee. "Excuse me, ma'am," he said. "But did you make that sign?"

"Yes," she said, puzzled.

"Well, it has a slight error. *Midnight* is one word."

"Oh, thank you," Saratoga said, and she corrected her mistake.

❧ THIRTEEN ❧

Inside the crowded club, the Woollybear Jugband was playing a toe-tapping tune. While one Woollybear swished the stiff bristles of her body against a washboard, the other blew into a jug.

Johnny St. Claire directed Leon, Spider Kane, and Little Pickles to a corner table near the stage. As he lit down on his chair, Leon looked about anxiously for the Bald Buzzer and his hornets. All the dancing bugs looked rather odd in their various outfits. They were wearing everything from dark turtlenecks to bright Hawaiian shirts. None, however, looked like he could be the wicked robber-fly.

"So tell me, Johnny," Spider Kane was saying. "How is your dad? I haven't seen Earl in a blue moon."

"I'm afraid Dad passed on a while ago," said Johnny, bowing his head.

"Oh, I'm very sorry to hear that," said Spider Kane. "Earl St. Claire was a remarkable bass player."

Johnny smiled and sighed. "Well, he certainly admired you, too, sir. I'd love to play music with you someday."

"Well, maybe you can sit in with us tonight, Johnny."

"Tonight? That would be terrific. What are you going to play?"

"Oh, I thought we might try something new," said Spider Kane. "Maybe a jazz arrangement of an old nursery song, like 'The Hokey-Pokey,' 'A Tisket, a Tasket,' or 'I'm a Little Teapot.'"

Leon quickly caught Little Pickles's eye. What did Spider Kane have up his sleeve? But Little Pickles only shook her head in bewilderment.

"Great," said Johnny. "You know, I heard an old song just this afternoon that had a nice melody. Now what is it called? Oh yes, 'Ducks on the Millpond.'"

Spider Kane stared at Johnny St. Claire with burning interest. "Ah, indeed," he said slowly, "that is a very good song."

"'Ducks on the Millpond'?" squeaked Leon.

"Just where did you happen to hear it, Mr. St. Claire?" said Spider Kane.

"Well, it's an odd story. When I was taking a walk, I heard it coming from the hill behind the club. It sounded like a moth singing. You know, that sort of dusty, resonant kind of voice moths have."

"I know it well," said Spider Kane.

"Anyway, the singing had stopped by the time I got over the hill," said Johnny.

"And there was no sign of the singer?"

"Nope. There was just this old bee house."

"Bee house?" Spider Kane sat forward in his chair. "Did you say 'bee house'?"

"Yes, a cement bee house, built long ago by mortar bees. But the singing couldn't have come from there."

"Why not?"

"Because the place is abandoned. The door was locked with a heavy padlock."

"Ah...Perhaps the singing came from a wandering gypsy moth, Johnny."

"Oh, yeah, I didn't think of that. Well, I better get back to work. If I can help you out onstage, let me know."

"Will do, Johnny," said Spider Kane.

As soon as Johnny St. Claire left them, Leon grabbed Spider Kane. "That's the Hawk in that bee house!" he said. "He sang 'Ducks on the Millpond' to the Tailor Ants of Borneo! That's how he got his tapestry!"

"Oh, my!" said Little Pickles.

"Yes, I know," said Spider Kane. "I imagine he was singing to the other captives, trying to lift their spirits."

"Well, why don't we go out there and find them?" cried Little Pickles.

But Spider Kane was now staring at the entrance of the club, where Saratoga D'Bee was greeting new arrivals. "In good time, in good time..." he murmured.

"But why wait?" said Leon.

"Because we must catch our enemy first," Spider Kane said. "And in order to do that, I want to try a little experiment."

"But, Mr. Kane," said Leon. "I think we should hurry out to the bee house! What if Raymond Johnson never arrives? What if we're just wasting precious time?"

Spider Kane turned to Leon. "I believe Raymond Johnson is already here, Lieutenant," he said softly.

Little Pickles gasped.

"Here? Where?" said Leon.

"Please be patient with me," said Spider Kane. "I am loath to reveal suspicions without proof. We'll just play our music...and see if it uncovers the beast."

A shiver went through Leon.

But just at that moment Jumbo Nightcrawler began shouting from the stage: "Ladies and gentlemen, please give me your attention!" The huge worm looked dazzling in the pink spotlight. Wearing a flowered silk vest and a black bow tie, he stared fondly at the crowd while he puffed on his fat cigar. "At this time I'd like to bring out a fellow who's never performed in public before. He's a little nervous. He's a little scared. So let's give him a big hand to make him feel welcome."

The bug audience started cheering and clapping enthusiastically. After a moment an odd figure stepped out from behind the curtain.

"Mr. Walter Dogtick, ladies and gentlemen!" shouted Jumbo. *Mr. Walter Dogtick!*

"What in the world?" breathed Leon. He couldn't believe his eyes. Walter Dogtick was dressed in a very expensive-looking outfit. He wore a gold tuxedo and on his feet were four pairs of shiny black patent leather shoes.

As the audience applauded, Dogtick moved into the pink spotlight. "Hi, folks," he said shyly. "This morning I was feeling mighty blue. I was feeling so blue, in fact, that I decided to end it all in the Garden Creek."

The audience groaned sympathetically.

"But then by the creek, a miracle occurred that changed my whole life," said Dogtick. "And I decided to live."

The audience applauded Dogtick's decision.

"And now I'd like to sing a little song that describes what happened to me. I call it 'The Dogtick Blues.'"

Dogtick closed his eyes. He took a deep breath. Then he began singing in a slow, bluesy voice:

"My baby she left me one dark, foggy night.
My baby she left me one dark, foggy night.
She said, 'Mr. Dogtick,
You don't love me right.'

"I found a sailor ant a-cryin' near the creek.
I found a sailor ant a-cryin' near the creek.
He said, 'Take all my treasure.
Mercy's all I seek.'

"Gonna hire me a detective t' find my baby in
the fog.
Gonna hire me a detective t' find my baby in
the fog.
When detective finds my baby,
We're gonna live high on the hog."

The crowd cheered as Dogtick bowed again and again.

Spider Kane turned to Leon and Little Pickles with a look of utter amazement. "There's a lot going on here tonight," he said, "a lot going on…"

"Thank you, Mr. Dogtick," said Jumbo Nightcrawler. "You did an excellent job."

When the audience quieted down, Jumbo leaned toward the mike and said, "Now we have a really big treat for y'all. My friend Johnny St. Claire tells me that we're about to hear some of the best jazz music east of the Mississippi. Let's give a big welcome to the Doctor Legs Trio!"

"Come on, friends," said Spider Kane, standing. "Let's go weave our web." Then he started limping toward the stage with a bewildered Leon and Little Pickles hurrying after him.

⋞ FOURTEEN ⋟

Leon felt frantic as he sat down at the piano. He was desperately afraid Raymond Johnson was about to swoop down and grab the three of them.

But Spider Kane did not seem worried at all. "Key of F," he called to Leon. Then he lifted his clarinet to his lips and began a lively tune. Leon began plunking his piano, and Little Pickles tapped her drum.

Spider Kane's playing was astonishing. His high notes seemed to noodle about the air, then soar into the atmosphere. The audience went wild, screaming and cheering.

After a moment Spider Kane put down his

horn and sang in a deep, springy voice:

> *"Hello, Bugland,*
> *Call me Doctor Legs.*
> *I say, Hello there, Bugland,*
> *Call me Doctor Legs.*
> *I'm gonna get all you bugs*
> *Out dancing on the floor.*
> *I'm gonna leave all you bugs*
> *A-wantin' more 'n more.*
> *I say, Hello, Bugland,*
> *Call me Doctor Legs!"*

As Spider Kane went back to his clarinet, Leon studied the cheering crowd. Jumbo Nightcrawler and Johnny St. Claire seemed enthralled with the spider's performance. For once the worm's foul-smelling cigar had gone out. And Johnny St. Claire was wiping tears from his eyes.

Saratoga D'Bee, however, seemed completely unaware of the band as she greeted bugs at the door. Leon wondered if she was anxiously awaiting the arrival of Raymond Johnson.

Suddenly Leon nearly fainted with fear. A

hornet glided into the supper club. Then another. Then another and another. Saratoga D'Bee seemed oblivious of the hornets as she kept welcoming other new arrivals.

Meanwhile, the four grisly gang members glided to different parts of the room. One hovered near the ceiling. Another hung near the juice bar. Another settled at a back table, and the fourth loitered near the stage. Leon desperately looked about for Raymond Johnson. But he didn't see anyone he thought could possibly be the dreaded robber-fly.

When the song ended, the audience applauded wildly. With his eyes closed, Spider Kane mouthed, "Thank you, thank you."

Leon quickly flickered over to him and whispered, "Hornets are here!"

Spider Kane came to attention and scanned the room. "Ah…" he said as he spotted the hornet gang. Then he looked at Leon. "Now's the time," he said mysteriously.

Spider Kane turned back to the cheering crowd. "Thank you, thank you," he said above the roar. "It's so nice to play here tonight. At this time I'd like to ask a wonderful musician to sit in with us for a song or two. Let's have a big hand for Mr. Johnny St. Claire!"

"Yay!" the audience screamed.

Johnny grinned and buzzed forward.

"Welcome, Johnny," said Spider Kane.

Johnny saluted Spider Kane with his trumpet.

"And as a special treat, I'd like to add another member to our little musical family," said Spider Kane. "Perhaps if we give her a big round of applause, Ms. Saratoga D'Bee will join us up here too."

The audience clapped with enthusiasm, but Saratoga shook her head frantically. "No, thank you, I can't!" she called. "I have to meet someone soon."

"Oh, come on up, Ms. D'Bee," called Spider Kane. "Don't be bashful. We need you up here. Come give us a song."

But the bee kept shaking her head no. "I see our great singer is very shy," Spider Kane said to the crowd. "But if we all clap loudly enough, maybe we can convince her to join us."

The audience clapped and chanted, "D'Bee! D'Bee! D'Bee!" Leon felt angry and frustrated. Why was Spider Kane being so persistent in trying to get Saratoga to join them? Time was being wasted!

Saratoga still shook her head vigorously, until a couple of enthusiastic bog beetles scooped her up and began hustling her through the crowd. Spider Kane turned to the band and said, "'Hokey-Pokey'!" As the beetles delivered the bee to the stage, the band began a jazzy intro to the old nursery song.

Though the audience cheered madly, Saratoga D'Bee did not look at all happy. She straightened her blond wig and adjusted her rose-tinted glasses. As the band began playing a hot version of "The Hokey-Pokey," Spider Kane stepped in front of her and sang:

> *"Put your right wing in,*
> *Take your right wing out,*
> *Put your right wing in,*

And then you shake it all about.
You do the Hokey-Pokey
And you turn yourself around;
That's what it's all about."

Leon could tell Saratoga was fighting the urge to sing and dance. As Johnny St. Claire blasted away on his little trumpet, her head twitched in rhythm with the song. Then as Spider Kane started the second verse, Saratoga began softly singing with him in her deep, buzzy voice:

"Put your left wing in,
Take your left wing out,
Put your left wing in,
And then you shake it all about.
You do the Hokey-Pokey
And you turn yourself around…"

Suddenly Saratoga D'Bee threw back her head and screamed: "THAT'S WHAT IT'S ALL ABOUT!"

As the band kept playing, she seemed to lose her mind. She started spinning all over the stage. Then she picked up the mike and screamed:

"Do the Hokey-Pokey, folks!
Do it! Do it!
Put three legs in!
Take three legs out!
Put three legs in!
And shake them all about!
SHAKE IT! SHAKE IT!
SHAKE IT!
AHHHHH!"

Johnny St. Claire tooted away on his little trumpet. Leon banged the piano, Little Pickles pounded her drums, and Spider Kane blew his clarinet. As the band played, Saratoga D'Bee danced wildly around the stage. She buzzed forward. Then she zipped backward. All the time she was screaming and shaking. It was the strangest and most compelling performance Leon had ever seen.

"Flap those wings! Do the Hokey-Pokey!" she shrieked.

Leon looked at Spider Kane and noticed the spider staring with burning interest at Saratoga as she jerked her head from side to side and darted here and there. As she darted, her apple-green cape billowed out from her body, exposing two vibrating wings.

Leon was puzzled to see a big grin break out on Spider Kane's face. "Yes! Yes!" the spider exclaimed.

Then Saratoga screamed, "That's what it's all about!" and collapsed to the stage floor. The audience went crazy.

But Saratoga raised her head once more and screamed even louder, "That's what it's all about! That's what it's all about!" And she collapsed again.

The audience went insane with joy. Bugs were banging into the ceiling and turning flip-flops on the dance floor.

Saratoga raised her head once more, screamed, "THAT'S WHAT IT'S ALL ABOUT!", then collapsed for good.

Spider Kane took over. He began moving around the center of the stage, and as he moved, he played a scorching solo. His clarinet filled the room with wild, haunting sounds. One moment he sounded like a baby crying, then a rooster crowing, then a train whistling in the night.

The crowd screamed and applauded. Only Leon seemed to notice that while Spider Kane was playing, he was also pulling thread from the pocket of his tuxedo jacket. Cobweb thread!

Spider Kane danced around and around Saratoga, and as his hot-sounding music snaked through the room like a blue flame, he wove a nearly invisible web around her. By the time he finished his solo, his cobweb thread completely surrounded her.

Standing outside the sticky web, the spider lowered his horn, and staring at the bee, he began to sing:

"'Will you walk into my parlor?'
Said the spider to the fly."

Saratoga looked up, startled, and began rising from the floor.

"Is your true name Saratoga?
Or is that a great big lie?"

Saratoga buzzed toward the front of the stage. But she pulled back just before crashing into the web thread that separated her from Spider Kane.

> *"Is it really Raymond Johnson —*
> *Here with your hornet crew?"*

Saratoga D'Bee buzzed frantically to either side of the stage, but she found herself completely trapped. Spider Kane leaned toward her and sang:

> *"Well, it's E. M.'s pretty parlor, friend,*
> *That you have stepped into."*

"AHHHH!" Suddenly, in the middle of the stage, Saratoga D'Bee went berserk. She buzzed around in circles. Then she yanked off her rose-tinted glasses. She yanked off her blond wig. She was bald! She was a HE! And foaming at the mouth, he shrieked, "YES! YES! YES! I AM THE BALD BUZZER! THE GREATEST CREEP ON EARTH!" Everyone gasped, then began screaming. Even Leon screamed at the sight of the aging bald robber-fly with the huge bug eyes.

The Bald Buzzer rushed blindly toward Spider Kane. But since the spider was still on the outside of his web, the fly was instantly caught by the web's sticky strands and held prisoner. "Get him! Get that spider!" the Bald Buzzer screamed to his henchmen.

But the cowardly hornets all zipped out of the club, escaping the doom of their leader. As the Bald Buzzer screamed with rage, he became hopelessly entangled in Spider Kane's web.

The club broke into pandemonium.

"Call for the Waterfront Police!" Spider Kane shouted at a stunned Jumbo Nightcrawler. "Tell them you've captured Raymond Johnson!" Then he rushed over to Leon and Little Pickles. "Let's get out of here," he said. "Quick—before anyone discovers who we really are."

On their way out of the club, Spider Kane stopped in front of the imprisoned robber-fly. He reached through the web and yanked the gold-key necklace from around his neck. "Congratulations, Raymond," he said softly. "You've still got it in you. That was a splendid performance."

"AHHHHH!" the fly screamed.

Spider Kane gave him an elegant salute, then took off with Leon and Little Pickles rushing after him.

❧ FIFTEEN ❧

At the door of the club Spider Kane halted. "Wait!" he said to Leon and Little Pickles. "We have to help Dogtick!" And he led the way through the screaming crowd to the back of the club, where Walter Dogtick was cowering in his little outfit. The old tick was pressed against the wall, looking quite frightened and confused.

"Mr. Dogtick!" shouted Spider Kane. "Come with me!"

"Oh, no, please, don't kidnap me!" Dogtick cried.

"I'm not a kidnapper, Wally. I'm your old friend Spider Kane."

"Spider Kane, the detective?"

"Shhh!" said the spider, putting a hand over Dogtick's mouth. "Yes. Come with me and I'll take you out of here. Hold on to the back of my coat!"

"Oh, thank you, thank you," said Dogtick.

"Follow us!" said Spider Kane to Leon and Little Pickles. Then he led them all through the hysterical mob out into the stormy night.

Once they were outside, Spider Kane hurried through the rain with the group to a leaf awning behind the supper club. There, Leon and Little Pickles hung in the shadows so Dogtick would not recognize them.

"Now, Wally!" shouted Spider Kane above the din of the wind-driven rain. "We don't have much time. Tell me quickly—how did you afford this fancy outfit?"

"I told you in my song, Mr. Kane!" shouted Dogtick. "I came across a sailor ant hiding in a cove on the creek bank. He had a bag full of gold, and he just gave it to me!"

"And where do you suppose he got this bag of gold?"

"I don't know, he didn't say!"

"What *did* he say?"

"Well, he said something about being a traitor. Then he pushed the bag into my hands and took off, calling for a thunderbolt to strike him dead."

"Did that behavior not seem a little suspicious to you?"

"No—yes," said Dogtick, dropping his head. "I know I should have called the police or something, but I was desperate! I need money to hire a detective to find Pupa Leafwing."

"I have good news and bad news, Wally. The bad news first: Recently a United Ant Charities cargo ship was robbed of its gold shipment. Hearing your story, I've now concluded that the sailor ant guarding the gold was the thief himself! But once the deed was done, the ant began to feel great guilt and remorse, and he abandoned the gold to you on the bank of the creek. Therefore I'm afraid you will have to hand your gold over to the United Ant Charities."

Dogtick moaned with disappointment.

"But now the good news, sir," said Spider Kane. "As you know, I am a detective, and I am about to lead you to Mrs. Pupa Leafwing."

"What? What?" cried Dogtick.

"Yes! Come along!" said Spider Kane. Then with Leon and Little Pickles following, he helped Dogtick over the dark hill behind the supper club. As the four of them approached a thick clump of thistle, they heard the plaintive song of the Hawk coming through the storm:

"Ducks on the millpond, a-geese in the
  clover,
A-fell in the millpond, a-wet all over."

Spider Kane led the group through the high grass until they came upon the cement bee house built long ago by mortar bees.

"Now, Walter," the spider said in an urgent whisper, "this is what you must do. Take this key and unlock the padlock on that door. Then open the door and call for Mrs. Leafwing. When she comes out, grab her and rush her to safety. Others may come out with her, but ignore them. You must take Mrs. Leafwing away as quickly as possible."

"You mean *I'm* going to be the one to save her?" said Dogtick.

"Yes. And you can take *all* the credit, Wally."

"Oh, wow. Thank you. Thank you!"

"You're quite welcome. But you must promise me one thing, my friend."

"What?"

"That you will never reveal to her or anyone else that I am Doctor Legs—or that I helped you tonight."

"Why?"

"Because I must keep my various disguises secret for my detective work. Surely you understand."

"Ah, yes, sir. Yes, sir."

"Good. Now go and save your sweetheart, Wally," said Spider Kane, and he handed him the gold key.

As Dogtick stumbled toward the bee house, Spider Kane turned to Leon and Little Pickles. "Follow me," he said, and he quickly led them into the tall grass, where they hid.

As Dogtick struggled with the padlock, Leon could hear the Hawk's voice over the rain:

*"Ducks on the millpond, a-geese in the
    clover,*

*Jumped in the bed, and the bed turned
over."*

With great difficulty, Dogtick finally hauled open the heavy wooden door. "Pupa?" he called into the bee house.

"Yes?" came a tired, frightened voice.

"Come out, precious. I'm here to save you!" shouted Dogtick.

"Wally? Wally, is that you?" Then La Mère fluttered out of the bee house into Dogtick's arms. "Oh, Wally! You saved me!"

"Dat's right, precious."

As the two clung to each other in the storm, Leon's eyes filled with tears. He was very glad that his mother and Dogtick had each other.

"Let's get outta here!" Dogtick shouted. "Come on, carry me, sweetheart!" He climbed onto La Mère's back, and the two of them took off into the storm, winging it away from the wild side.

"Come!" said Spider Kane. And he rushed with Leon and Little Pickles toward the bee house. As Rosie, the Hawk, and Mimi all stum-

bled out into the night, everyone grabbed everyone and shouted with joy:

"Rosie!"

"Leon!"

"Mimi!"

"Hawk!"

"Spy!"

"Little Pickles!"

"Thank heavens!"

"Thank goodness!"

"You saved us!"

"Let's go!"

❧ SIXTEEN ❧

The stormy weather had come to an end, and
dawn winds had scattered the clouds. Sunlight
streamed in through the windows as the latest
recording of the Hot Bugs of France filled the
Hawk's living room with jazzy swing music.

"No one suspected the theft of the ants' gold
was an inside job," Spider Kane was saying to

the group as he relit his pipe. "But as all ants are basically good at heart, the thief's conscience eventually got the best of him."

"But tell us, Spy," said Rosie. "How in the world did you ever suspect Saratoga D'Bee was really Raymond Johnson—the Bald Buzzer?"

"From the beginning I sensed something was not right about that bee," said Spider Kane. "But then three things in particular made me very suspicious."

"What?"

"The first was a misspelled word. On her sign for the talent show, Ms. D'Bee had incorrectly spelled the word *midnight* as two words. That's exactly how it was spelled on the blue notes you all received."

"Oh, I didn't even notice that," said Leon.

"What else, Spy?" said Rosie.

"Well, when Johnny St. Claire told us about the abandoned bee house, I realized not only that you were all being held prisoner there, but also that Ms. D'Bee had been lying to us."

"What do you mean?" said Leon.

"She told Miss Pickles she did not know where the captives were. But when Johnny mentioned the bee house, I remembered Saratoga's song, 'The Bee House Stomp'—in which she'd sung: 'Put them in the *bee house*, just for fun.'"

"Oh, yes! Of course!" said Leon.

"It seems Raymond Johnson's vanity about his clever songwriting got in the way of his better judgment," said the Hawk.

"Indeed," said Spider Kane. "The third thing that tipped me off about Saratoga was her gold-key necklace. Johnny mentioned a padlock being on the door. Most locks come with keys. And the nearest key at hand seemed to be the one dangling from Ms. D'Bee's gold chain."

"Oh, goodness," said Little Pickles. "I admired her necklace, but I never made that connection."

"But before I made my move against her, I needed absolute proof," said Spider Kane. "All this evidence did not prove that Ms. D'Bee actually *was* Raymond Johnson. It only indicated she was working more closely with him than she'd

119

led us to believe. Therefore, to prove that the two were one and the same, I decided to entice the bee into performing for us."

"Why?" said Rosie.

"Well, in his singing days Raymond Johnson was known for his wild renditions of simple nursery tunes, such as 'A Tisket, a Tasket' or 'I'm a Little Teapot.' So when I began to suspect Ms. D'Bee might actually be Raymond Johnson, I decided to try an experiment. I thought that if I could persuade Ms. D'Bee to sing 'The Hokey-Pokey,' she might abandon herself and perform in Raymond Johnson's inimitable style."

"So that's what you were up to!" said Leon.

"Oh, Rosie, you wouldn't have believed how bizarre that performance was," said Little Pickles. "And yet how wonderful…"

"And then of course, the performance also disclosed a bit of scientific evidence that probably no one but myself would have gotten," said Spider Kane.

"What was that, Spy?" said Rosie.

"When Ms. D'Bee's cape billowed out from

her sides, I saw she had only a single pair of wings. Though bees look a great deal like robber-flies, bees have *four* wings whereas robber-flies have only two."

"Oh, that's why you cried, 'Yes!' when she was dancing," said Leon.

"Precisely," said Spider Kane.

"Wonderful job, Spy!" said the Hawk, and everyone clapped for Spider Kane's brilliant detective work.

"Now tell me this, Spy," said Rosie. "Why would Raymond Johnson disguise himself as a singing female bee in the first place?"

"I think the old boy was trying to kill two birds with one stone," said Spider Kane. "He disguised himself as a female bee singer first so he could scout the waterfront for clues to the missing gold without being recognized. But even more than that, I think he secretly longed to perform again."

"And the setup at Jumbo's allowed him to do just that," said Rosie.

"Exactly," said Spider Kane. "When Johnson

—disguised as Ms. D'Bee—told Miss Pickles he'd finally found his true home at Jumbo's, I believe he really meant it. In fact, I believe much of what he said to Miss Pickles was sincere. I'm afraid the poor fly was defeated only by the 'creep' within himself."

A hush fell over the room as the Order of the MOTH contemplated the tragedy of Raymond Johnson.

"What will become of him now, Spy?" said Rosie. "Years in Bug Prison, I suppose?"

"He deserves it, Rosie. But I would hate for such a tremendous talent to go to waste. I think, therefore, I'll talk to my good friend Judge Bagworm and see if a life sentence of community service might not be a better punishment for Raymond. Perhaps he could use his musical skills to inspire wayward youth."

"Here, here," said the Hawk, leading the group in a brief applause.

"Well!" said Spider Kane. "Our mission has come to an end. Though I'm afraid we'll receive no credit for it." The spider chuckled. "I imagine